☆ Star-Time ☆

Life on a film set is nothing like Charlotte had imagined. She has no script and no one seems certain what she's expected to do. Even her sixteenth century ringlets keep dropping out.

Jo Henry, the director, reminds Charlotte of an animal tamer, but all the crew and cast love him (when they're not hating him). All, that is, except the conceited Big Star, Red Smith, who is determined to get Jo Henry off the film.

RACHEL BILLINGTON

☆ Star-Time ☆

Illustrated by Alice Englander

A Magnet Book

First published 1984 by Methuen Children's Books Ltd
This Magnet edition published 1986
by Methuen Children's Books Ltd
11 New Fetter Lane, London EC4P 4EE
Text copyright © 1984 by Rachel Billington
Illustrations copyright © 1984 by Alice Englander

Printed in Great Britain
by Richard Clay (The Chaucer Press) Ltd,
Bungay, Suffolk

ISBN 0 416 52120 7

☆ Contents ☆

To Chloe with love

Chapter 1

CHARLOTTE WINS THE PART

Charlotte sat on the very edge of her chair. Even so her feet didn't quite touch the floor. She bent over and just managed to make contact with the tip of her toes. It was a very high chair, the sort of chair especially designed to make children nervous. It was certainly succeeding in her case.

She moved the curtain of her long fair hair and looked sideways. First she saw her mother's legs. They wore brown shiny boots and tapped the carpet impatiently. Then she saw the swinging legs of another girl. Then another mother, then a third girl and a third mother.

They were all waiting to be auditioned for a part in a film. The film was called *Ladies and Gentlemen* and was set in 1641. The silence in the room was terrible. When one of the girls sneezed, everybody jumped and her mother produced a huge handkerchief with a look of terror.

There were two doors in the room. One they had come in through and the other led to the office where they would be interviewed. A fourth girl was in there at the moment. They had all watched her go in. She had red hair parted into two

curly bunches. She had freckles dotted across her nose and huge turned-up blue eyes. She looked just like a film star in the making. She didn't walk, she danced. The word 'cute' came into Charlotte's mind.

'Ugh!'

'What?'

Charlotte had spoken aloud. Her mother gulped – everybody else stared, and the door burst open to the office.

Out tripped the cute red-head.

'Thank you. Thank you,' said a woman with a clipboard. She looked round the room in a harassed way. 'Charlotte Leopold, please!'

Charlotte's mother who was called Lily Leopold leapt out of her chair. 'Here we are!'

Charlotte wished her mother didn't get so excited about things. She got off her chair rather slowly and walked, with deliberately ordinary steps, towards the office. She had decided to be as unlike the red-head as possible – even if it

did mean she wasn't chosen to be a film star.

The office had a huge desk in it. It was so huge and dark that Charlotte could hardly see the two men behind it. Then one of them bounded round. He had thick, dark hair, a sun-tanned face and gleaming green eyes. He wore a tasselled leather jerkin and high leather boots. Although he was not very tall he seemed to fill the room with his energy. He reminded Charlotte of an animal tamer.

He shouted 'What's your name?'

'Charlotte Leopold' said Charlotte rather crossly. The woman had that written on her clipboard.

'Have you had any acting experience?'

Charlotte didn't answer at once. She was taking in the other man behind the desk. He had the biggest, reddest face she'd ever seen. It was poised above a spotted bow-tie. He looked, she thought, like a performing porpoise. A mean performing porpoise, she added to herself as she noticed his tiny reddish eyes.

'No,' said Charlotte, remembering the question. The porpoise had just put a long cigar into the middle of his face.

'But darling! All that at school. And at home. She never stops acting.' Lily pressed forward eagerly. 'That's why the school suggested her.'

'But you haven't been to drama school,' the animal tamer continued to address Charlotte.

'You said you didn't want acting school types,' interrupted the woman with the clipboard in an aggrieved voice. 'I've been scouring London schools.'

The red face heaved behind the desk. 'How many more Jo Henry? I've got a lunch date.' Smoke came out with the words in strong-smelling gusts.

The animal tamer whose name was Jo Henry didn't answer. He walked round Charlotte. She kept still, confident with her newly-washed hair and freshly ironed dress. She even wore new shoes.

'Do you want to be in the film?' he asked abruptly.

'Yes,' said Charlotte.

'Why?' he stopped and crouched down, face to face.

Charlotte looked calmly into his bright green eyes. She knew the answer to that one. 'Because I like pretending to be someone else. I feel better then. I feel more myself.'

Her mother stirred behind her protestingly. 'Darling, what a silly thing . . . you can't feel more yourself when you're acting someone else . . tell them about the school panto . . . .'

But Jo Henry stood up, cutting her off. He swung round to the performing porpoise. 'O.K.' he said in his loud decisive voice, 'I'll have this one.'

The woman with the clipboard sighed in a relieved way. The porpoise heaved about and put the cigar onto an ashtray. He rose to his feet. He was tall as well as broad. He bared his teeth in what was presumably intended as a warm smile. He held out an oddly small hand across the desk.

Mrs Leopold and Charlotte stared at it wonderingly.

'Shake hands with your producer,' said Jo Henry in a mocking sort of voice, 'Bernard B. Bagelman.'

Charlotte went forward nervously. But Lily got there first. 'Do you mean she's got the part?' she cried.

Bernard B. Bagelman held onto her hand. His little fish-eyes winked. 'Your daughter, my dear lady, is on her way to stardom.'

Mrs Leopold looked as if she might faint. Bernard B. Bagelman squeezed her hand tenderly. 'You are a very charming and talented woman. I can see that. Like mother like daughter.'

'Oh, yes!' breathed Lily.

Behind her Jo Henry and Charlotte exchanged an understanding glance. They would never behave so foolishly.

'Elizabeth!' cried the producer breaking loose from Mrs Leopold. He came round to the front of the desk and addressed Charlotte. All of a sudden it was as if *he* had chosen her.

Charlotte looked at Jo Henry. He said, poker-faced, 'That's your name in the film.'

'My little Elizabeth!' Bagelman bowed and leered.

Charlotte felt some response was needed. She held a fold of her dress in either hand and bobbed down in a neat curtsy. 'Thank you very much, sir.'

'Delightful.' The producer turned to Jo Henry. 'What a joy to be present at the birth of a new star!'

'Quite,' said Jo Henry in a dry kind of voice.

'Hold on.' The woman flipped through the pages on her clipboard. 'She's in less than a third of the scenes.'

'A great light from a little flame,' said Bernard B. Bagelman and turned his back on them.

After that they went home.

They went home in the producer's car. It was so big that Charlotte could not see its front and back at the same time. It took two whole meter spaces outside the producer's office.

'A car fit for a queen!' cried Mrs Leopold. She was talking to the chauffeur, Charlotte supposed. But he was far too grand to answer. When he shut the door after them he gave a disapproving grunt as if to say, 'And who might you be to ride in my car?'

Charlotte and her mother sat back in the cream leather seats with gracious expressions. They felt too elegant to talk.

Even so as they approached home, Mrs Leopold bounced on the edge of her seat. Then she pressed her nose against the window. 'I do hope they're watching out for us.'

Charlotte had three older sisters and two younger brothers. They were twins. This made her family very big. Much too big for their little house. Her father was away being captain of a tanker two thirds of the year. But when he came home Charlotte thought the walls of the house might pop like a balloon. She imagined all of them and all of their furniture strewn over the street. Charlotte played games of 'let's pretend' so much of the time that she didn't always know the difference between what was really true and what she was pretending.

'Number Ten Laburnum Gardens,' grunted the chauffeur, slowing down the car.

'Oooh! Look. There they are!' The whole front window of their house was crammed with children. Mrs Leopold waved back with an arm like a flag.

Charlotte looked too but she didn't wave. She loved Mrs Leopold very much but sometimes she made her feel as if she, Charlotte, was the mother and her mother was the daughter.

She thought about the afternoon and how Jo Henry had understood what she meant about being more herself when she was pretending to be someone else. She had never told anyone that before. She knew that was why she had won the part. It was most satisfactory.

'Charlotte's won the part!' screamed Mrs Leopold, although no-one in the house could hear. 'She's going to be a film star!'

Chapter 2

JO HENRY VISITS

Charlotte didn't feel like a film star. She lay face downwards on her bed. Ned was sitting on her back and Fred on her legs. They were bouncing her up and down like a trampoline. Ned and Fred were twins and only three so it didn't hurt at all, in fact it was fun, but not at all like being a film star.

'Stop it, Ned! Stop it, Fred!'

Iris, who was Charlotte's eldest sister, lay reading on the next bed. Usually books made her deaf so Charlotte was quite surprised when she looked up and said, 'Buzz off, boys.' Of course it had no effect but it was nice of her all the same. Perhaps she did seem different, after all, more grown-up, more graceful.

'You are a baby.' Pansy and Marigold stood in the door to the bedroom. They were Charlotte's next to eldest sisters, and were inclined to be critical.

'Mum says you'll bring the ceiling down and we've got to take you to the tube station to have your photograph done.'

They all knew the big machine in the station with its little

swinging curtain behind which lights flashed but none of them had ever used it. Charlotte rolled out from under Ned and Fred and followed her sisters downstairs.

'Here's the money and make sure it works first time.' Mrs Leopold was ironing, otherwise she might have noticed that Charlotte looked very very untidy.

Pansy and Marigold didn't notice either until they reached the machine and were drawing back the green curtain. Then Pansy said, 'You do look a mess.'

'Like a wild witch,' agreed Marigold.

Charlotte looked in the mirror on the side of the machine and saw they were quite right. Her hair straggled in all directions all over her face. She said, 'I don't want my photo taken.'

'Of course you do,' said Pansy roughly. 'You might be playing a witch in the film. It might be just the right look.'

'I don't want to be a witch.' Charlotte was near tears.

'Sshh.' Marigold smoothed the hair from her face and tied it with the ribbon. 'Now you look lovely.'

Charlotte sat on the little round plastic seat behind the curtain and waited for the light to flash. But she didn't smile for the camera. She thought how sad it was having three sisters older than her who called her 'baby'. Ned and Fred who really were babies had a nice time bouncing about and never caring if they were told off. She was stuck in the middle, neither old nor young. Really she was very unhappy. As the light flashed for the fourth time, a large silver tear popped out of Charlotte's eye and quivered on the edge of her cheek.

When they got home Mrs Leopold had finished the ironing and was laying lunch. She wiped her hands and took the photographs eagerly.

'Oh, dear.' She sighed. 'Look at your hair. And what's that mark on your cheek?'

'It's a tear-drop,' said Charlotte, studying the photograph with some pride. She had thought tear-drops were a kind of magic that wouldn't come out on photos.

'We told her to smile,' said Pansy.

'No, you didn't,' said Charlotte. 'You said I was a witch. That's why I cried.'

'Well, they'll have to do. The director's coming to pick up two this afternoon. For your licence.' Mrs Leopold stuck them up on the mantelpiece.

At this moment, the doorbell rang. (Or rather sang since they had recently installed a bell which played 'Life on the Ocean Wave'.) Mrs Leopold rushed to the living-room window to see who was there.

'Oh dear. Oh dear. Lunchtime too.' She tore off her apron and stuffed it behind a cushion.

Charlotte stared at the front door. It was patterned glass

and she could see two dark figures behind it. She thought they were burglars or murderers or murdering burglars or burglaring murderers. One of them held a long black gun.

Mrs Leopold opened the door. Jo Henry stood there with a friend. 'We expected you this afternoon.' And since that sounded cross she added with a rainbow twirling smile 'Such a lovely day!'

Actually, it was beginning to rain. Charlotte saw the gun was a gentleman's handbag.

'I thought you were murderers,' she said.

'Don't sound so disappointed,' replied Jo Henry energetically.

They went into the living-room. Lily Leopold produced the photographs with many apologies. Jo Henry turned to Charlotte: 'Say after me: "You look so elegant, mama."' He sat down and stared at her. 'Fire ahead.'

Charlotte saw that she was to act. At last. She brushed back her hair, opened her blue eyes very wide and pursed her lips. 'You look so . . .' But before she could attempt the 'elegant' the doors burst open with an explosion of noise and laughter, 'You look so elephant, mama. You look elephant! Elephant! Elephant!'

It was Ned and Fred with Pansy, Marigold and Iris chasing behind them. They rushed round and round the room like wild animals in a circus ring.

'Crack your whip!' shouted Charlotte excitedly, remembering how she'd thought Jo Henry was like an animal tamer.

But it was her mother who drove them out of the door. 'We'll have lunch,' she said shutting the door firmly.

The living-room was very quiet.

'Don't you want me to say the elephant line again?' Charlotte asked politely and then catching the second man's eye began to laugh. She hadn't really meant to say elephant. Well, only half meant to.

'What a little joker!' Jo Henry did not look very pleased.

He turned to his friend. 'Where is Ruby? You told her 12.30 didn't you?'

Charlotte took the cushion from behind her back. It was very pretty, all pinks and yellow, soft and round. She realised she was very hungry. Her tummy was quite flat. The front of it would soon touch the back. She could smell lunch from the kitchen. But the men took no notice of her, talking as grown-ups do as if there was no-one else in the room.

Lifting the skirt of her dress, she slipped the cushion up to her tummy. She patted it proudly. Twins, she thought. Twin girls. Lucy and Kate. She'd look after them and they'd do everything she told them. She sat back, smiling.

The two men stopped talking. One said, 'Just look at her. A real mother-to-be.' The other nodded. 'You can see why I wanted her in the film.'

Pleased to have their attention again, Charlotte smiled at them peacefully. This was interrupted yet again by 'Life on the Ocean Wave'.

'Ruby,' exclaimed Mr Henry.

A very fat lady wearing a huge hat with a pink feather came into the room. Lily Leopold followed anxiously behind. Charlotte put her babies behind her back and leant on them.

Ruby said, 'Helloaaah Joeee!' and kissed him. Charlotte noticed him shiver violently as the feather tickled his neck. 'And where is my little Elizabeth?'

'I'm Charlotte.' She stood up primly.

'Ha, ha, ah!' Ruby crouched down in front of her. Tassels on the edge of her huge pink dress spread to the floor. Charlotte thought she looked like a round table with a tablecloth and a head perched in the middle of it. 'Do you like dressing up?'

'Oh, yes!'

'Well, I've got a car full of dressing-up clothes. Just for you.'

When Ruby stood up again, Charlotte saw she did have

legs but they were very like table legs with little dark button boots on the end.

'Will I be dressed as a table, too?' she asked with an innocent smile.

Chapter 3

A GRAND SEND-OFF

'We'll just have to ring up and say you can't be in the film after all!' Mrs Leopold's face was pale and her forehead resembled a corrugated roof. Charlotte knew the signs.

She lay on the floor and cried so hard and fast that the carpet became wet and uncomfortable. She moved a little in order to be able to carry on crying. 'I want to go. I need to go. I hate Ned! It's always Ned. Why's it always Ned?'

Ned had mumps. His face had swollen up in the middle of the night. He had woken them all with his screams. Poor Lily had sat up with him till dawn and then called the doctor.

'The doctor said there was a lot of mumps about,' wailed Charlotte. 'He didn't say he'd got mumps.'

'Oh, dear. Oh, dear. And they've ordered that special car to pick you up.' Mrs Leopold looked just as disappointed as her daughter. 'Maybe we could put off telephoning till tomorrow.'

'Oh yes. Oh yes. Oh yes!' Charlotte was off the floor in a moment, arms wound round her mother's neck.

'But even if it isn't mumps it must be something, so I

could never leave him to be your what is it they said?'

'Chaperone,' said Iris who'd come into the room.

'That's right. Chaperone. Twenty-five pounds a day for doing nothing.'

They sat round dully. Everyone had been excited by the thought of Charlotte's adventure – even if the big girls were jealous, too.

It was quite a relief when the doorbell rang through the house.

'Perhaps it's the doctor again to say it's not mumps just simple over-eating,' said Charlotte hopefully. 'Like a squirrel puffs out his cheeks for the winter.'

'It's the summer,' said Iris.

'And Ned's not a squirrel,' said Pansy.

In fact it was Lily's sister, Cheryl, at the door. Cheryl was as languid as her sister was energetic. She was tall and dark and thin and was not married and had a different job every time she called. She thought the Leopolds were the worst-behaved family in the world but it didn't stop her calling round most days.

'Out of a job again,' Lily said as she entered the room.

'Couldn't stand the supervisor,' Cheryl flopped down into the only comfortable chair. 'How's our star today?'

This gave Charlotte the chance to start crying again.

'Now what have I said?' Cheryl looked at her with surprise.

'Ned has mumps.'

'Might have mumps.' Charlotte's sobs diminished. Her hair felt like a wet flannel around her face.

'So I couldn't be her chaperwhatnot. Twenty-five pounds a day down the drain.'

There was a pause. Even through her hair Charlotte felt something happening in the room. She looked up.

Cheryl leant forward and said with a nonchalant shrug. 'My time's my own. I'll be her chaperwhatnot.'

'Oh, you angel! You darling!' Charlotte (who had

previously considered her aunt less attractive than an earwig or a worm, both of which she hated) now flung herself on her with expressions of undying love. 'Oh, you, you – golden swan!'

'That's all right, dear,' Cheryl pushed her off and smoothed down her skirt. 'Anything to help your mother. I'll give you ten per cent commission, Lily?'

'If Ned hasn't got the mumps,' said poor Lily Leopold in a resigned voice. She had been very much looking forward to going.

Ned didn't have mumps. He had toothache. Charlotte laughed unsympathetically when the truth was discovered.

But even so Lily wouldn't leave him. Now that there was an alternative chaperone she didn't really see how'd she ever planned to leave the boys for days on end.

Cheryl was only too happy to oblige.

The film car arrived very early in the morning. The sun had not yet risen high enough over the row of houses facing the Leopolds' house to get in their windows. Even so no one in the whole house was asleep.

Charlotte thought she had not slept all night but Pansy said you can't snore without sleeping and her snores had woken her, Pansy, up. To which Charlotte had replied huffily that film stars didn't snore and besides, if you had twenty rags in your hair you might make sounds of agony.

'Agony! Agony,' cried Pansy. 'Listen to her, she thinks she's on a film set already.'

'Now, now. Let's see about your hair.'

'Oooh, yes,' Charlotte sat down obediently. The night before they'd had a call from the film hairdresser who'd told Lily that Charlotte needed ringlets and she must twist her hair up with rags.

Charlotte imagined how beautiful she would look with golden curls cascading down her back. 'Oh dear.' Lily took out one rag and then another. 'I don't think this is right.' She held up a strip of hair doubtfully. 'It looks more like rats' tails than ringlets.'

Luckily, before Charlotte could become too upset the film car's chauffeur rang the door-bell.

Fred and Ned (despite his toothache) crowded at the window shrieking with excitement. Cheryl, usually so leisurely, pounded up the stairs.

'The car's here! It's here!'

Cheryl was dressed all in scarlet including long red shiny boots. She also wore a lot of golden jewellery which banged and clattered along her arms and beside her sharp jaw-bone. She had got up earlier than anyone in order to crimp her dark hair into a thousand tight little curls. Noticing Charlotte and Lily staring at her, she flung her arms above her head in model pose.

'Don't I look just perfect for the films!'

'Perfect,' agreed her sister weakly. There was no point in having a row at this late stage. Charlotte was not so tactful.

'You look just like a cannibal queen!' she cried. 'You know, the sort who jump round the cauldron and eat each other.'

At once Cheryl turned on her ferociously. 'And what do you think you look like, little miss clever? Like a pale little mouse with two dozen mouse tails hanging round your scrumpy little nozzle!'

This was true. Charlotte looked at herself critically in the mirror.

'The film people will have to fix you, that's all.' Mrs Leopold pushed her off the chair. 'You ssh, Cheryl. And do answer that door.'

The poor chauffeur who had been ringing 'Life on the Ocean Wave' till it sounded as if the ship was sinking, was now hammering on the door. Above his head Ned and Fred had managed to open the window and were leaning out shouting comments.

'I don't know why those girls can't do it,' grumbled Cheryl

but she went down all the same.

'A very good morning to you!' Charlotte heard her say sweetly as she opened the door and the chauffeur, fist raised for one final pound, fell face forward into the house. As he fell his arms hit the gong standing nearby and set up a great booming. All the children rushed onto the landing and peered over the bannisters. '--------!' and '--------!' and '--------!' screamed the poor chauffeur.

It was not a very dignified start to Charlotte's film career. Things did not improve even when they reached the car. Lily rushed out at the last minute and thrust an unwinding toilet roll through the window. 'You never know with these film people!' she called cheerfully.

Then, at last, they were off. Cheryl was not speaking to Charlotte (owing to her Cannibal remark) and the chauffeur was not speaking to Cheryl (owing to her causing him such a nasty fall). But, nevertheless, they were off.

Charlotte tossed back a dangling rag and laid a hand on Cheryl's scarlet knee. 'The point is,' she said in her nicest voice, 'I like cannibals.'

'Grrh!' replied Cheryl and gnashed her teeth so angrily that Charlotte really thought she was about to eat someone. Not her, she hoped.

Chapter 4

ENTER 'LADIES AND GENTLEMEN'

They found the film company in the middle of Windsor Great Park. The chauffeur who was still sulking, stopped the car beside a group of lorries and said without turning round, 'All change!'

Cheryl who was now in high spirits, jangled out of the door and waved two fingers at him, 'See you around, dearie!'

Charlotte scrambled after her. It was still early and the trees were shrouded in a depressing grey mist. It was cold too and in her hurry she'd forgotten a coat. She shivered violently.

'What's this, then? Little Orphan Annie before she meets her millionaire.' It was Ruby, the out-sized costume lady. This time she was wearing a velvet table-cloth. 'Come along now and I'll turn you into Lady Elizabeth.' Charlotte's hand was taken in a hand as puffy as dunlopillow.

'And what about me?'

Ruby surveyed Cheryl. 'You don't look as if you need much dressing-up. I'd get yourself a cup of tea. The van's over there.'

Ruby led Charlotte into a small caravan. In fact it was more like being inside a wardrobe than a caravan because clothes hung in every available space. She had to push between a red velvet cloak and a black satin dress to get inside at all. It was very warm and there was a delicious smell of musty age. Charlotte was reminded of her mother's wedding-dress kept in blue tissue under her bed. She thought she would like to stay hidden among the soft clothes all day.

'Now where is that flaming sprigged muslin? Excuse the Italian.' Ruby snuffled among the clothes like a huge brown velvet mole. 'Ha! Ha! Got you! And the petticoat! Now if I can just find the boots and hat . . .'

The clothes directly in front of Charlotte were swept aside like a curtain and she found herself face to face with Ruby.

'Everything present!' she cried triumphantly. 'Now off with that nasty old bit of Tricel.'

Charlotte knew just what it felt like to be a doll. Legs and arms stuffed into holes as if they had no feelings. Waistband snapped shut, skirt twitched, boots buckled. It all was done in a matter of seconds.

Ruby stood back against a dress of purple silks. 'You'll do. No point in trying the hat. Now for Hair and Make-up. And don't forget to hold your skirt up. Grass-stains are the devil. Excuse my Polish.'

Charlotte had no idea what she looked like. Or who she was. She wished she'd dared to ask for a mirror. Outside the dark caravan, she blinked and screwed up her eyes. The sun had broken through the mists. But she had hardly gone a few paces before Ruby was pushing her up the steps to another caravan.

'Upsi-daisy and don't let them turn you into Miss World 1641.'

In front of Charlotte the door opened and a glorious apparition appeared. It had pink hair with silver streaks, white face with black eyebrows, and a suit apparently made of tiger skin.

'Oooh!' gasped Charlotte. 'You must be the star!'

The apparition laughed. 'Stars are nothing like so exciting. I'm the hairdresser, George. But you can call me Gorgeous like everyone else does.'

This new caravan was like an Aladdin's cave. It was lit brilliantly by dozens of light bulbs which shone round a row of mirrors and reflected back into the room. Jewels hung about the walls. Emeralds, diamonds and pearls in clusters as big as a fist. As Charlotte's eyes became more used to the light she saw behind all the glitter a row of heads, displaying beautifully curled heads of hair. It made Charlotte feel a bit creepy. The caravan suddenly seemed less like Aladdin's Cave and more like Bluebeard's Chamber.

'Take a throne, dearie, and we'll see what we can do with this horrid mess you've got growing out of your head. Your mother's talents obviously do not lie in the crimping direction.'

Charlotte did not quite understand what he meant but the mention of her mother made her feel sad and faraway. A large tear-drop formed at the back of her eye but before it could fall, Gorgeous was upon her.

'Well, we are a pretty thing. In the raw as it were.' Like lightning, he slid the rags out of her hair and gathered the whole mass into his hands. 'A bit of the heated what-nots and Jo's your uncle! All you have to do is keep perfectly still or there'll be grilled little girl for breakfast.'

He gave Charlotte such a ridiculous pouting look in the mirror at the same time that she found herself laughing and the tear drop quite forgotten.

'That's better,' Gorgeous smiled approvingly. 'The film isn't all tragedy. At least it's not supposed to be. Though the way he's going . . . .

As Gorgeous talked, as he did all the time about the problems of the film, he wound Charlotte's hair round heated tongs until in no time at all she had the shiniest most bouncy ringlets in the world.

'Oh thank you, Gorgeous!' cried Charlotte. 'I look really, well, gorgeous.'

'Until the damp gets you. Now where's Miranda Watson-Poxson for a touch of colour on those cheeks?'

Gorgeous shouted 'Miranda W. P.' at the door of the caravan while Charlotte admired herself in the mirror. She saw now how very pretty her dress was. It had frothy lace at the neckline and round her elbows. She gave herself a seventeenth-century smile.

Her peace was broken by a rustle and a bustle as a woman in full period costume pushed Gorgeous aside and burst into the caravan. 'This wig is made of barbed wire and leaden weights.' Plumping herself down in the chair next to Charlotte she raised her be-ringed hands to her head and pulled the whole mass of yellow curls off her head. Underneath was a little pleat of dark hair. Charlotte stared with amazement.

She seemed to notice Charlotte for the first time. 'And who are you, staring hard enough to make your eyes pop.'

'Oh, no. I mean I'm Charlotte.'

'Ha! Well, I'm the star in this film and you're sitting in my chair. If you look on the back you'll see it says Helen Wittering. And that's me.'

'Oh, I'm so sorry . . .' Charlotte leapt to her feet.

'Come on, Helen. Pick on someone your size.' Gorgeous patted Charlotte comfortingly.

'I'm sorry.' Helen leant back in her seat. 'What a beast I am. Come here, you little darling. I expect you're going to play my daughter.' She drew Charlotte towards her.

'Are you Lady Clarissa?' Charlotte asked timidly.

'So they tell me.'

'Then I am your daughter. I have to say, "You look so elegant, mama."'

Helen laughed and gave Charlotte a little kiss. 'I see you've had a script.'

'Which is more than most of us,' put in Gorgeous.

'Oh, no. I just had to say that line to Mr Henry,' explained Charlotte.

'Mr Henry. I like that.' Helen laughed again but with a rather nasty expression. 'Isn't that his right name?'

'After making me stand in the dew for two hours doing fanny all I wouldn't like to say what his right name is.'

At that moment there were more bounding noises at the door and Jo Henry himself shot in.

'My darling!' To Charlotte's surprise Helen immediately raised her face for a welcoming kiss.

'Helen, angel! What you've been through!'

'Nothing, nothing at all.'

'The dew, the waiting, the lights. You should be rechristened Patience!'

As they embraced warmly, Charlotte thought she had a lot to learn about film people. However Jo Henry now turned his energy on her. 'My little Elizabeth!' He turned to

Gorgeous. 'Can you loop in a couple of ribbons? I want her over-the-top pretty.'

'There is a hat?'

'With that head of hair. Forget it.' He chucked Charlotte under the chin. 'Now for breakfast.' And he was gone again.

Breakfast turned out to be the most exciting picnic Charlotte had ever had. Tables and chairs had been set up in the sun near the van. The oddest assortment of people were eating. Some wore seventeenth-century costume with cloaks and swords and huge hats with feathery plumes. But that, after all, was expected. It was the non-actors who looked odder, several of the men, although it really wasn't that hot, already stripped to the waist. And then there was Gorgeous with his pink hair and Ruby in her table-cloth and Jo Henry in his ring master's outfit and Cheryl, of course, in her scarlet.

Cheryl found Charlotte a seat and brought her a bacon sandwich and juice. She was in higher spirits than ever. 'You can eat and drink anything, any time and all absolutely free!' she exclaimed. 'No wonder these film types are so deliciously beefy.'

Charlotte was glad to see Cheryl happy but inside herself worried about when they would use her. It was all very well to sit in the sun eating but that's not why she was there.

'I wish someone would tell me when I'm going to be Elizabeth,' she said sadly.

'Oh, that's easy,' Cheryl nudged her neighbour who was a small frightened-looking man said to be the writer, 'What's the next scene?'

The little man shrugged and then looked as if he might cry. 'What makes you think I'd know?'

'I thought you were the writer.'

'Hurrumphgrrumph!' He made a sound like an angry hippopotamus.

'I do apologise,' said Cheryl a little huffily.

'We could ask Ruby,' suggested Charlotte as the walking table-cloth swayed past them.

'Too late,' sighed Cheryl. 'For the communications industry, they're very uncommunicative.'

'What?'

'Nothing dear. Eat up your sandwich.'

Charlotte was just chewing her last juicy mouthful when a heavy hand fell on her shoulders. She turned to see a young man dressed in camouflage over which ran an assortment of wires and boxes and microphones and head-phones.

'O.K. Elizabeth,' he said in a loud voice. 11.30 pm call. I'm Digger. I'll send someone to collect you. Get Gorgeous to check you over at 10.30.' Then he was gone again.

Cheryl and Charlotte looked at each other with excitement. Then Charlotte's face fell. 'But what am I going to be doing? I can't say "You do look elegant, mama" over and over again.'

Cheryl looked sideways at the writer slumped over yet another cup of coffee.

'He must know something about the script,' she whispered, though he seemed beyond hearing. 'You can't write something without knowing anything about it. You ask him.'

'Excuse me, sir,' began Charlotte politely. The writer looked up blearily. 'I wonder if you know what I'll be doing in this film. I'm playing Elizabeth, Lady Clarissa's daughter.'

'Are you? Are you now,' the writer rumbled.

'Perhaps you might know what I say?' Charlotte encouraged him.

'Say? Words, you mean.' The writer leant forward with a conspiratorial expression. 'I'll tell you a secret. Except it's a secret to no one. The director on this film has no interest in words. Pictures. That's what he likes. Moving pictures. So don't think I can tell you about your words. I can tell you what I wrote, what I sweated blood over. But that's another matter altogether. If you want to know what you're doing, ask make-up or costume, they know more than I do!'

By the end of this speech the writer had risen from his bench and was glaring over Charlotte's head. He then walked off towards a patch of uninhabited trees. Charlotte felt sorry for him but disappointed too. They were no nearer knowing what she was to do.

'What we need is a script, I'm surprised they didn't give your mum one in the beginning. We'll just have to wait,' said Cheryl, not looking too unhappy about it. 'Want another juice?'

'No, thank you.' Charlotte was regretting the bacon sandwich. 'You know, I can actually feel the curl dropping out of my hair.'

As it turned out Gorgeous had 'put in' Charlotte's ringlets three more times before she was sent for by Digger. They had also had a coffee break and a lunch break and the sun which had been so high and bright was now more going than coming and when it came it was through the trees and a dark golden colour.

'Hurry along now. They're all waiting for you.'

Charlotte thought that was a bit of a cheek since she had been waiting all day. However she ran along as fast as she could, which wasn't very fast as she had to hold her skirt up to stop her falling over and hold the bottom of her ringlets to stop them uncurling.

She arrived panting in a glade among the trees. Huge lights were turned onto the centre. In their brilliant light she could see Jo Henry dancing about in what appeared to be uncontrolled rage. At a short distance a very tall man in a black velvet cloak stood with his arms folded.

Charlotte stopped nervously. 'Come on!' Digger pulled her impatiently. In a moment she found herself in the centre of the lights, facing Jo Henry. He stopped dancing about and looked at her very closely.

'Nice,' he said, 'Very nice indeed.' And to Charlotte's surprise he gave her a wide cheerful smile.

'Now,' he continued, 'I want you to stand here.' He pulled her over a few yards. 'And then, we'll be ready to go!'

Charlotte stared at him. There was something very wrong about all this. She looked round wildly for support but no-one was near. Only the great glaring lights. Now even Jo Henry had disappeared behind the lights. She puffed out her chest and cried as loud as she could, 'But what am I supposed to DO?!'

The disembodied voice of her director replied to her, 'You DO exactly what I tell you to.'

Chapter 5

CHARLOTTE TAKES A STAND

Charlotte stood in a daze. Since Jo Henry had put her in position a very small man wearing tartan trousers had come up with a tape measure which he'd asked her to hold. He'd then run off into the distance with the other end. Then a very large man wearing shorts came right up to her face with some sort of glinting box. Then they'd both disappeared and she'd be left alone again.

But when she happened to glance at the sky which was filled with the prettiest pink and golden clouds, a very cross voice shouted, 'Would you mind keeping quite still, *please!*'

Charlotte couldn't help thinking this wasn't the life of a film star as she'd imagined it. One of her feet was starting to go to sleep and she could feel her ringlets uncurling yet again. Just as she thought this, Gorgeous darted towards her and expertly flicked the ends of her hair round his fingers before flashing off again. He was followed by Ruby who pulled her dress up on the shoulders and stuck in a couple of pins.

'O.K.' said Jo Henry's voice. 'Now I want you to walk

three paces forward looking at the ground . . . Walk! I said, not run.'

In her eagerness to be on the move, Charlotte had rushed towards him. She stopped just as suddenly.

'Right. Back to your mark and start again.'

To Charlotte's surprise she saw a white stripe had appeared on the grass.

'O.K. Forward . . . slowly now . . . As if you're looking for something . . . hold it there. How was that?'

'Useless. The sun's going in and out like a yo-yo.' This was the cross voice, who Charlotte rightly supposed to be the cameraman. 'Another few minutes and the shadow of the trees will hit her anyway.'

'So we try somewhere else?'

'Unless it's a wrap?'

Charlotte did not understand what they were saying but did not dare move. She thought that if she knew who she was supposed to be, what sort of girl Elizabeth was, then the whole thing would be much more enjoyable. Then it would be like the kind of play-acting she'd described to Jo Henry in the beginning. She was very disappointed in Jo Henry.

So, since no one paid any attention to her, she began to repeat first softly and then louder, 'Who am I? Who am I? Who am I?' Soon she was having great fun. It seemed to be the best moment of the whole day.

Then, without any warning, there was a clicking noise and the lights stationed round her went dark. She could now see the crowd of people, including Gorgeous and Ruby and Cheryl and even the writer, skulking behind a tree. It made her feel rather silly. She was considering where she could hide when Jo Henry reappeared. He took her hand with an elegant gesture and kissed it. 'You were perfection, my dear. You looked so sweetly sad.'

Charlotte realised this was her chance. 'I was sad. I am sad,' she cried. 'I'm sad because I don't know the story we're playing. And I don't know who I am. And do you know I tell my horrible little brothers more about what's going on than you tell me. Or, as far as I can make out, tell anyone!'

Jo Henry looked at her with total amazement. As he gulped, apparently lost for words, Charlotte noticed that a lot of the film people had edged closer. They were all silent, waiting, presumably, for his explosion.

'So you see,' continued Charlotte, feeling she might as well say everything now she'd started, 'It's really no good me staying if that's how you want it because I won't act your Elizabeth well and it's just a waste of both our times!'

Jo Henry closed his mouth. And then opened it again. Then he closed it again. Charlotte patted his arm. 'I expect I've got a very little part so it won't matter if I go.' To her right she saw Cheryl's face mouthing 'No'. She looked away but added, 'Quite frankly it's not at all what I expected that day we met in Mr Bagelman's office.'

She took a step away and clasped her hands, 'So there you are! Take it or leave it!'

A noise rose around her. It was clapping. All the film people, stood in a close circle now, were clapping loudly. Charlotte was delighted. Smiling and blushing, she bobbed her little curtsey, first one way and then the other.

As the clapping died down, Jo Henry found his voice. 'Well,' he whispered. (He'd only found a very small voice). 'Well. I think we'd better have a tea-break.'

'Yes,' agreed Charlotte approvingly. 'Being sad is a very thirsty business.'

'Tea-break!' shouted Digger (the man with the box of wires and headphones). 'We'll start at 5 with the new set-up.'

Charlotte sat in the make-up caravan holding a script of 'Ladies and Gentlemen'. Written on the outside cover in gold letters was 'The property of MS CHARLOTTE LEOPOLD'. Jo Henry had presented it himself with a charming smile, 'For the greatest little actress I've seen for a long time.'

He then rather spoilt the effect of this by glowering round the caravan at the other occupants and snarling out of the side of his mouth, 'But don't think this gives you lot any additional rights.'

'Poor Jo Henry,' said Charlotte smugly when he'd banged the door. 'He does seem so upset all the time. From now on I shall be extra nice to him. Like my mother tells me when Fred keeps pulling my hair.'

No one commented on this good resolution so Charlotte opened the script to start reading. The only trouble was that she couldn't understand it. The words were fairly easy but they were laid out all over the page in such a funny way that she didn't know where she was. For the sake of her dignity she did her best to look as if she was reading but she didn't think anyone was convinced, even though she made a show of turning over the pages. Eventually she gave a big sigh and laid it down, 'I'm just too tired to read it!'

'Of course you are, dear,' said Gorgeous sympathetically. (He was now doing Charlotte's ringlets for the fifth time with the same good humour he'd done them at first.) 'Get Miranda educated-middle-class-Watson-Poxson' to read your bits out to you. That'll be much more fun.'

Despite these insults Miranda W. P., who was the make-up girl, took the script cheerfully. She flicked through it.

'You've got quite a bit in it,' she said.

'Of course she has,' said Cheryl importantly.

'But what was I doing in the middle of the trees?' Charlotte asked intently. 'What was I looking for – if I was looking for something?'

'Well – ' Miranda hesitated and flicked through more pages. 'There's a bit here says "Elizabeth is terrified. Not caring she is still in her nightclothes, she jumps out of the window and runs over the dewy grass . . ."' she looked up doubtfully, 'You weren't in your night-clothes, were you?'

'No,' agreed Charlotte. 'And anyway I didn't jump out of a window.' She paused. 'I hope it's not a very high window.'

'That would be another shot anyway,' Miranda tried more pages. 'There's a mention here of you with your mother in the garden.'

'But my mother wasn't there.'

'So that's no good. Here's one where you see a lone horseman galloping by.'

'I suppose I could have been looking at the hoofprints,' said Charlotte without much hope.

'Of course it might be one of Jo Henry's unprogrammed extras,' Miranda made a face.

'And they're plenty of those,' agreed Gorgeous.

'I think it's very odd,' complained Charlotte, 'that none of you know the story. If you knew the story it would be perfectly easy to find where I came in.'

'You see we do it all in bits,' explained Miranda very kindly under the circumstances. 'That's how films are made. Scene number 10, followed by scene number 204.'

'But how do you know all the bits will fit together?'

'Quite often they don't,' giggled Gorgeous.

'The director knows. At least, he's supposed to know.'

'Well, I think it's a very silly way to go about things,' said Charlotte severely. 'It's like trying to make a puzzle without the picture to follow.'

'And usually we do the end at the beginning. And the middle at the end. And the beginning at the middle.' Miranda smiled at Charlotte's cross face.

'I've never heard anything so bonkers!'

Miranda laughed and shut the script. 'I suggest you take it home tonight and get your mother to read it and tell you the story. Then tomorrow you can tell us.'

'That is a good idea. I say, I couldn't have another of those pink and yellow cakes, could I?'

Charlotte thought that Cheryl had been right at the start, the best thing about filming was the food. It was just as well she had decided that because a few minutes later, Digger came along to announce that she would not be needed again that day.

Cheryl and Charlotte sat back in the chauffeur-driven car. The chauffeur still wasn't speaking to Cheryl. He was being nice to Charlotte however, and had wrapped up six pieces of the pink and yellow cake for her mother and her brothers and sisters. He had been amazed at the numbers necessary, and said, 'Your father must be quite a chap,' so Charlotte explained he was on a tanker at sea most of the time at which he snorted and said, 'Looking for a bit of peace and quiet, I've no doubt.' So then Charlotte decided she didn't want to talk to him.

After a while driving along thinking their own cross thoughts, Cheryl said, 'That was a funny sort of working day. Tomorrow I'll bring Snakes and Ladders and Scrabble and my manicure set.'

Charlotte didn't comment. She was fighting the temptation to eat her mother's piece of cake. After all, she was always saying how she must diet. She took a tiny nibble.

'Do you think we get paid a full day even though you finish early?'

'I don't know.' Charlotte evened up the side of the cake.

'I don't think they actually filmed you at all. I mean I was quite near the camera and it didn't seem to whir or click or anything. Really, there seemed to be a lot of wastage. People hanging round not doing anything.' Here she gave a meaningful look at the chauffeur's back.

Which he obviously caught in the rear view mirror for he immediately turned round (they were in a traffic jam at the time) and barked, 'That just shows you don't know the first thing about filming! The point is you need a well-drilled army ready to spring into action at a moment's notice.'

'A well-drilled army,' repeated Cheryl snootily, 'more like a gang of gypsies. Still, I suppose it does give employment to those who would otherwise be supported by the state.'

'That's true, anyway,' said the chauffeur, glowering at Cheryl.

Luckily at this point the traffic moved on and he had to turn back to the wheel.

Meanwhile Charlotte discovered she had managed to eat the whole of the pink and yellow cake. 'Oh dear,' she wailed, 'I only meant to even it up.'

'Never mind,' Cheryl patted her hand. For some reason her argument with the chauffeur had put her in an excellent humour. 'Poor Lily should never touch cake with hips her size.'

'That's what I thought.' Charlotte was consoled.

'Besides, she'll be far too excited with all your news to want to eat.'

Chapter 6

RAIN AND STARS

Lily Leopold held the script in her hands. 'Oh, Charlotte,' she whispered, 'this is special. It's as if you were in a book.'

'Not really, Mum,' objected Pansy. 'I mean it doesn't say her name anywhere.'

'But it says Elizabeth and that's who she is.'

'But it's not . . .'

'Read it Mum, go on!' interrupted Charlotte who had been waiting for this moment through Ned and Fred's bath-time and bed-time and Cheryl's leaving and their supper. (She, of course, hadn't room for another thing).

'Wait a moment while I get my glasses.'

Charlotte sat expectantly. It was funny, she thought in passing, that now her ringlets weren't needed they were staying in beautifully. Marigold and Pansy had been most impressed.

'Ladies and Gentlemen,' read Mrs Leopold from the cover.

'We know the title already,' cried Pansy.

'I think it's funny to make a film about Public Lavatories,' laughed Marigold.

'Sshh, girls.' Mrs Leopold gave Charlotte a reassuring smile. 'We know it's only jealousy, don't we, dear. Now I shall begin.' She held the script up to her face. "1641. A lone horseman gallops along a dusty road. He looks behind him as if fearing he is being chased. Suddenly there is a sound behind a bush. The horse shies. The man is thrown" Lily stopped reading and raised her glasses on her head. 'I don't know. My eyes are so tired tonight. Iris dear, would you go on. The words do dart over the page so.'

So Mrs Leopold lay back, and although she was rather big for this, Charlotte climbed onto her lap and Marigold and Pansy sat quietly in the same big chair. And Iris read.

She read about Sir Joshua Ponsonby who was a loyal courtier to Charles I at the time when there were many plots against his life. About his beautiful wife, Lady Clarissa who was secretly plotting against her own husband. And, of course, about their daughter, Elizabeth, who was very beautiful and courageous and everything a little heroine should be. She saved her father's life not once but twice and at the end of the film forgave her mother on her death-bed. Her mother's death-bed, that is.'

'I'm glad you don't have to die,' said Mrs Leopold, wiping a tear from her eye. 'I do love a good story.'

'I've never been so tired.' Iris closed her eyes.

'You read it beautifully, dear.'

'It's 11 o'clock!' shouted Pansy suddenly.

Mrs Leopold couldn't believe she'd kept her girls up so late. 'That's what comes of no man around the place,' she said a little sadly. 'You lose track of time. Now Reggie would never let me behave so foolishly.'

'It is holidays, Mum,' pleaded Marigold.

'Not for Charlotte, it isn't. She's picked up at 7 again tomorrow. Isn't that what the driver said, Charlotte?'

But Charlotte was fast asleep. She was dreaming of galloping horses and floating lacy dresses and didn't even wake when her mother and Iris carried her up to her bed and undressed her. It had been a long day.

The next morning it was raining. Cheryl arrived covered in white plastic from head to toe. When the chauffeur saw her he said, 'Emergency Ward 205.'

'You are out of date.' Cheryl posed provocatively. 'Can't you recognise après-space-travel gear when you see it?'

Charlotte was so tired she curled up in the back of the car and went to sleep again.

When she woke up the car was stationary and she was all alone. It was still raining outside but not so heavily. Peering through the window she could see the vans and lorries belonging to the film. It all looked very wet and miserable. She decided to stay where she was till someone called her. She would pass the time by learning her lines from the script. Iris had marked them for her that morning.

The next time she looked up two men were standing near the car. One was Jo Henry dressed in a green oilskin and a deerstalker. The other was the large cameraman with the shorts and cross voice. He was wearing a cape over his shorts and holding a kind of spy glass up to the sky. 'It is clearing,' he said, 'the wind is moving the clouds off to the right. I'd say we'd be in business in under an hour.'

'We should set up then?'

'Yup. I'll get the brutes in now.'

Charlotte listened and watched eagerly. She thought that the cameraman, shorts aside, was like a wizard commanding the skies. And then, when he said about getting the 'brutes' in, she thought they were like two plotters out of the film. Who were the brutes?

'We've lost two hours.'

'You worry too much!' The wizard of the skies clapped Jo Henry on the back and moved off.

Charlotte sat up quickly and tapped on the window. Jo Henry turned round.

'Good morning,' she said brightly.

At first he didn't see her. Then he came over and opened the car door.

'Good morning,' she repeated. She thought he looked very sad, like her father when he had to go off to sea.

'Not very, I'm afraid.'

Charlotte searched for other subjects of conversation. It was odd to see him in no hurry. 'What are brutes?'

'Lights, Huge lights. Monsters to move around.'

'You're getting wet. Do you want to come in and have a game of something? Scrabble perhaps?'

'It's nearly stopped now.' He looked up at the sky worriedly but then slid into the car. 'You're a funny little girl, aren't you.'

'Certainly not.' Charlotte was affronted. She moved further from him along the seat. There was a pause. Then Jo Henry picked up the script.

'You've read it have you?'

'My eldest sister did. To all of us. Except my little brothers but they don't count. And of course my father's at sea.'

'And what did you think of it?' Jo Henry sounded casual but Charlotte could tell he really cared very much about the answer.

'We loved it,' she said enthusiastically. 'It kept us up ever so late because it was so exciting we didn't notice the time, and Mum cried a lot at the end when my mother, you know, Lady Clarissa died, even though she was bad in a way. We thought it was the best thing we'd ever read, better even than . . . ' Charlotte strived for something really good . . . 'better even than television!'

Jo Henry laughed. It was the first time Charlotte had seen him laugh and she thought it made his rather weaselly face look really nice. 'We'll have to make sure your mother and sisters come on the set sometime.'

They'd love that!' Charlotte frowned. 'Not Ned and Fred though. They'd wreck everything. It's not really their fault. It's just the wrecking age.'

'You see, this film is special to me,' Jo Henry leant

forward intensely. 'I'm trying to recreate in 80's language the great films of my childhood. The wonderful swash-buckling adventure stories of the 30's and 40's. *Captain Blood, The Corsican Brothers, Robin Hood, The Count of Monte Cristo.* For me it's a labour of love!'

'That is an exciting ambition,' agreed Charlotte in as adult a voice as possible. She was fascinated by his wildly glinting eyes. They were green and when he spoke seemed to spark like electricity. But suddenly his attention was diverted from her. He opened the door and leapt out. He whisked the deer-stalker from his head.

'It's stopped!' he cried. 'It's stopped raining!' Now where is everybody? We mustn't waste another minute!'

In a moment, the area round him was filled with running figures. All the characters of yesterday talking and arguing. One of them was table-cloth Ruby who handed Charlotte out of the car saying quite kindly, 'Enjoyed your forty winks, did you dear.'

46

'Yes. Thank you. Jo Henry kept me c . . . .' But Ruby was in too much of a hurry to listen. Charlotte saw Jo Henry disappearing towards the trees with his arms waving all over the place and she found it hard to believe he was the same person who had got into the car so quiet and sad. She thought film directors must have an extra amount of electric waves running through them. Perhaps he was recharging like batteries when he sat beside her. She felt very proud he had confided his deepest thoughts in her. Even if she hadn't quite understood it all. *Captain Blood* didn't sound a nice film at all. But she liked the idea of a 'labour of love.'

Charlotte bent down and picked a glove off the grass for the sixth time. It belonged to her father who had fallen from his horse, wounded, and crawled to a bush. In the next scene she would recognise the glove, see a bloodstain on it and start to look for her father.

But at the moment she was trying to pick up the glove the way Jo Henry wanted. Each time when she'd finished he'd shout 'Very good' and she would relax. Then would come the shout 'Just one more!' and she had to find her white mark again and Digger came up and clapped a bit of board in her face and off she went again. Six steps forward, see glove, two more, bend, pick glove up. Really, it wasn't very difficult. Every now and again Gorgeous or Miranda or Ruby darted in to pull or tug or pat. And once the tape-measure reappeared and once the large cameraman with the little box which she'd discovered was a light meter.

Of course it was very grand being the centre of so much attention. But it was tiring too. Her face began to feel stiff and however much she tried she couldn't show surprise when she saw the glove yet again.

'O.K. Cut and print the last take.' Jo Henry's voice boomed out and they'd finished for a moment. Someone brought Charlotte a chair and she sat down thankfully.

'These boots hurt,' she said to Ruby. 'I think they were

made for someone with only four toes.'

Ruby didn't laugh. 'Those flaming boots – excuse my Swedish – are a perfect copy of an early seventeenth-century design,' she snapped.

Charlotte sat alone on her chair. Cheryl, she assumed, was drinking coffee somewhere. She looked round at the trees and up at the sky. She felt a light touch on her face. It was starting to rain again. She felt very sad. Tears started from her eyes and joined the raindrops on her cheeks. She had not acted well. She had let Jo Henry down. Everyone was disappointed in her. That's why she'd been left alone.

'Whatever are you doing sitting in the rain?' Gorgeous was dashing across the grass. He wore a transparent pink plastic mac which matched his hair. His shoes were covered by large galoshes painted with pink and turquoise clouds. The sight of him cheered Charlotte even though he was cross. He began to bundle her ringlets into a plastic bag.

'I'm no good,' Charlotte cried. 'I had to do it eight times and then they cut it up.'

Gorgeous stopped with a surprised look, 'But you were wonderful,' he said, 'everyone thought so. Even Jo Henry and he avoids praise like measles. I thought since you're so matey, he was sure to have told you.'

Charlotte stopped crying. 'But why did I do it so often?'

'That was nothing to do with you. That was a lighting problem.'

'Ah,' Charlotte looked knowing. 'The brutes were playing up.'

'Oooh,' said Gorgeous admiringly, 'You *are* learning.'

'But what about cutting it up?'

'Not so clever, after all. That's just telling the cameraman to stop filming. Cut off. Do you see?'

Charlotte sighed. 'I'm not sure I do want to be a film star actress after all. It's all so complicated.'

Gorgeous gave her a friendly squeeze. 'Buck up now. We're taking an early lunch while it rains and I happen to know there is strawberries and cream for pudding!'

After lunch, Charlotte was introduced to the Big Star who was to act the part of her father. She was rather surprised to find he was American.

'Hi, there, Liz,' he said holding out his hand. 'So I'm to be your dad for a week or two. Now tell me, what does your own dad think of that?'

'He's on a tanker.' Since he was being so friendly Charlotte tried to be friendly back. But it did seem odd that she should have an American father. And really he just did not look historic. His teeth were so big and white and his nose so well, stubby and his hair such a brilliant yellow.

'Look at the way she's giving me the once over!' exclaimed the Big Star, showing all his teeth.

'Where's your manners, Charlotte?' reproved Cheryl who looked on him as if he was a God come down from Heaven. Apparently he was a very very famous film star.

'I'm sorry.' Charlotte blushed. His name was Red Smith. 'Were you always called Red?' she asked. 'I mean when you were a baby.'

For answer she found herself thrown up into the sky and then placed on one of Red's broad shoulders. 'How do you like that, my little chickadee!' His voice boomed in her ear.

'Oooh,' squealed Cheryl admiringly. 'Aren't you ever so strong!'

Charlotte tried to seem pleased, too, but actually she felt uncomfortable and undignified. Did he think she was the same age as Ned and Fred?

From her vantage point she saw Jo Henry approaching. He was talking, with his usual energetic hand movements, to the female star, Helen Wittering. She wore a white towelling robe, a striped towelling turban and huge green gumboots. Charlotte thought she would never get used to the odd clothes everyone wore. It was like being in a foreign land. Not that she had ever been to anywhere more foreign than Haverford West. They'd had a very wet holiday there, waiting for her father's tanker to dock.

'Father and daughter eh? Getting to know each other. That's good.' Jo Henry approached them shouting jovially.

He was not received in the same spirit. Red took down Charlotte and said in a cold drawl, 'I'd like a pow-wow, Jo, old fellow.' They went off together.

Helen watched them go. 'It's a rotten idea having a big star in a production like this,' she said as if to herself.

'Aren't you a big star?' Charlotte asked curiously.

'A mini English star with a steady line in T.V. serials.'

'But he's so super,' sighed Cheryl.

'He'd like to take over the film,' said Helen. And her face was so bitter that Cheryl and Charlotte decided not to say any more.

'Let's just hope Jo Henry's famous toughness will keep him at bay.' Helen turned and gave Charlotte a smile. 'I hear you did really well this morning.'

Charlotte thought how very kind everyone was turning out to be. Even when they had all sorts of terrible problems. It gave her a warm glow to be part of it all.

Suddenly grabbing at Helen's towelling, she gave her a big kiss.

'What's that for?' Helen laughed.

'It's because I think you're the Biggest Star in Outer Space!' Charlotte said and turned a slightly rectangular cartwheel to prove her enthusiasm.

'Mind your ringlets!' shouted Gorgeous.

Chapter 7

MR LEOPOLD RETURNS HOME

Charlotte had been filming for four days running and now she had a day off. It felt very odd to be sitting at home with nothing particular to do. It felt too ordinary.

'Can't we do something?' she whined.

Lily Leopold was doing the ironing, and didn't even hear her daughter. Or at least she didn't answer. Charlotte wanted to kick over the boring ironing-board. Instead she repeated 'Can't we do something? Can't we do something?' But there was still no answer. Admittedly Fred and Ned had set up a car race track on the floor and were either revving up or cornering, both extremely noisily.

'Can't we *do* SOMETHING?' screamed Charlotte.

Mrs Leopold looked up with a mildly surprised expression. 'What dear?'

'I'm so bored! I'm so bored!' Charlotte jumped up and down to make her point. 'Pansy and Iris and Marigold have gone out and left me and I can hardly play with the twins.'

Mrs Leopold looked down at the ironing again. 'You were sleeping and now you're supposed to be resting.'

'I'm not resting. I'm . . . I'm. . . .' Words failed to describe her restless boredom.

Her mother laughed. 'Have a drink and a biscuit, and we'll all go to the playground when I've finished this.'

'I don't want to go to . . .' began Charlotte but there was no use in going on. Her mother's attention was firmly back on the ironing again.

'I'm going to play outside,' she said.

'Don't turn the corner, mind.'

Charlotte stood in the middle of the pavement. It was midday and a warm sun reflected back from the stones. She tried to remember what they were doing in the film today. She thought it was a duel scene which she would have loved to watch. She kicked an old toffee paper and wondered if she could get any money from her mother for sweets. Almost certainly not. What was the point of earning huge sums of money if you weren't allowed to spend it. She made a mental note to find out exactly how much she made per day.

A car came round the corner. It stopped in front of the Leopolds' house. Charlotte who was a few yards further down watched curiously. A man got out lugging a big bag behind him. Charlotte suddenly realised she was watching her father coming home.

'Dad!'

Mr Leopold turned round and crouching a little, held open his arms. Charlotte ran as fast as she was able. Reggie whirled her round and round till there was no breath left in her body.

Then he set her down and said, as he always did, 'Well, well, well, you have grown. Quite the elegant young lady.'

Mr Leopold was the most satisfying father in every way but one. He was not very tall but very strong with thick muscles in his arms and neck. When Charlotte had been small enough to sit on his shoulders it was like riding an elephant. He had a very deep voice too like an elephant's bellow and when he laughed which he did often too the whole little house seemed to shake.

When Mr Leopold was home, Mrs Leopold had a permanent pink glow on her cheeks and looked nearly as young as Iris. The one thing wrong with him was that he was away two-thirds of the year.

'Mum!' screamed Charlotte, 'Dad's home!' They entered the house arm in arm, with smiles like soup-plates.

'Oh, no!' Lily put her hand to her mouth. Charlotte knew this was because she was wearing her old clothes and had not had her hair done. She always liked to look her best before her husband came home. 'What a surprise!' She looked almost cross.

'A nice one, I hope.' Reggie swept her into his arms. Charlotte looked on with approval. Meanwhile the boys had at last looked up from their cars and grabbed a trouser leg each. 'Dad! Dad!' they screamed.

A few minutes later the confusion grew as the older girls returned. It was all made more exciting by Ned and Fred's cars. Every now and again someone trod on one and found themselves whizzing across the floor, usually ending in a crash landing. Then Reggie put on the television 'to see what's been happening in good old England while I've been away', and Pansy and Marigold went to get some take-away pizza – since their father's last port of call had been Italy.

At last they were all sitting down quietly.

'So what's new?' Reggie took a large bite of his pizza. All eyes round the table turned to Charlotte.

Charlotte blushed and put down her pizza. 'I'm in a film,' she said, adding modestly 'Just a little part but it's very interesting.'

'I should think so,' bellowed Mr Leopold, and he put down his pizza. 'Lily, this calls for a celebration. Bring out the glasses.'

Everybody put down their pizza expectantly. On very

special occasions, a set of ruby glasses, which had belonged to the Leopold family when they had lived in Eastern Europe, were unpacked from blue tissue. They were then filled drop by drop with a sweet amber liquid by Reggie Leopold and a toast drunk to whatever occasion they were celebrating. Afterwards the smaller children tended to giggle and fall asleep.

Reggie, however, going on for a second and third glass, became even more expansive and told stories of his travels on the high seas.

Charlotte sighed happily. It was really wonderful to be the reason for the celebration. Last time it had been when Iris won prizes for French, mathematics and English at the end of term.

This time he wanted to know everything about the film. In the end Charlotte got the script and he took it to the big comfortable armchair where he always sat. Although he fell to sleep without actually reading any, Charlotte felt very proud to see her name in gold letters under his big strong fingers.

Just before he had fallen asleep he said he would come to watch the filming the next day.

Charlotte found it very strange to have her father in the chauffeur-driven car. Cheryl and she were always very quiet on the morning drive. The chauffeur and Cheryl were now talking but only just. They sounded as if they had a large plum stone in their mouths.

But Reggie threw himself into the front seat, introducing himself cheerily as 'our young star's father. You can call me Reggie. What's your name?'

'Bert,' said the chauffeur, trying to avoid Cheryl's eye in the mirror.

'And you're always on to this film racket, are you?'

'Film and commercials work is what my firm specialise in.' To Charlotte's surprise the plum stone had quite disappeared and soon the two men were talking away ten to the dozen.

Charlotte thought this might make Cheryl cross but on the contrary, she nudged Charlotte and winked in Bert's direction, 'It takes one to know another, eh?'

Charlotte did not understand this but smiled politely. She knew her father didn't like Cheryl very much because she'd once heard him saying to Lily, 'If she wasn't your sister I'd call her a tinsel-headed tart,' which Charlotte thought sounded a very nice thing to be but guessed from her father's voice was supposed to be nasty. Certainly they were very different kinds of people.

The point about Reggie was that he never changed his manner wherever he was or whoever he was with. While with Cheryl you never knew what she'd sound like next. Perhaps she wanted to be an actress too. Today she was wearing a purple and black sun dress with black sandals that criss-crossed like spiders all the way up her thin legs.

It was a lovely sunny day. When they arrived Bert took Reggie off for a coffee. Charlotte was rather relieved because she couldn't see him fitting into the little stuffy caravans. Everybody seemed in a very good mood.

Gorgeous said, 'So you're chasing horses today?'

'Am I?' asked Charlotte, who'd lost her way in the script again. 'I like your blue stripe.'

Gorgeous nodded his head down so she could see his hair better. 'It's going to be rainbow coloured. But they have to do one at a time or they'd run together.'

'Oh, it's lovely to be back,' sighed Charlotte. 'I don't know what I'd have done with myself at home if my father hadn't come back.'

'Listen to her,' crowed Miranda W.P. who had just painted Helen with a white face-pack. 'Bitten by the film bug already and still a baby.'

'I'm not a baby!'

'Sorry. Sorry.' Miranda tapped Helen's face so that it

rang like a bit of china. 'That'll do nicely. Now not a word for
fifteen minutes. You'll hear the alarum.'

'We shouldn't have much trouble with your ringlets, a
nice dry day like this.' Gorgeous gave Charlotte a friendly
pat. 'Off you go now.'

Charlotte danced down the steps of the caravan and
looked around to see where they were filming. She had
never felt jollier. Skipping and singing she made her way
towards the trees.

Suddenly she heard a pounding of hooves and out of the
trees burst a large black horse. On his back rode the huge
figure of Red Smith screaming and shouting, 'Help! Stop
him! I'm going to fall off.' Behind him ran the film's crew
also screaming and shouting, 'Help! Stop him! He's going to
fall off.' But none of them were anywhere near catching him.

Charlotte stood quite still and watched. Although she
hadn't liked Red Smith very much she could see it would be
awful if he crashed off and broke his leg. Horse and rider

were coming closer, the shouting louder. Red Smith's face
was bright red and he had lost the reins and both stirrups.

Then Charlotte noticed something. The sword which
Red wore on his left side was hanging against the horse's
side. At every step he took, it gave him a great wallop. No
wonder he was galloping so fast!

Charlotte took a step forward and cupped her hands.
Luckily she had developed a loud voice shouting at Fred and
Ned. 'Take off your sword! Take off your sword!'

At first Red didn't seem to hear through his fright but
then he looked at Charlotte. They were getting much closer
now. If he didn't stop soon they'd be in among the lorries
and caravans and that would be dangerous.

'Take off your sword! It's hurting the horse!'

Red understood. Holding onto the mane with one hand
he tried to unbuckle the sword with the other. Charlotte
could hear their panting now and see the scarlet inside the
horse's flared nostrils.

There was a clatter and a thud. The sword dropped to the ground. The horse gave an almighty buck, throwing Red round his neck and then stopped still. Red gave a groan and slithered off onto the ground. The horse's whole body heaved. His eyes rolled. His coat was as wet as if he'd been for a swim. There was a white lather where the sword had rubbed.

Charlotte took a little step forward. They had stopped only a few yards from her.

'Are you all right?' she asked.

Red groaned. But it was quite a lively, angry sort of groan so she decided to leave him and talk to the horse. He let her come right up to him and pat his wet neck. She felt he was trembling. 'Poor little thing,' she whispered, stroking his soft nose.

'Poor little thing, nothing!' groaned Red Smith from the ground.

'It wasn't his fault. It was your . . . .'

Perhaps luckily, they were interrupted at this point by the rest of the crew panting up to them.

'Are you all right? Are you all right? they cried.

'Would I be lying on the ground if I was all right?' Terror had obviously put Red in a very bad temper.

'But have you broken any bones?' Jo Henry looked as if he rather hoped he had.

'How do I know? I'm not a doctor, am I?'

Charlotte noticed a couple of the boys who pulled the brute lights around were trying to hide their laughter. This made her cross. The poor horse. 'You're all very unfeeling,' she said severely, 'The poor horse has had a terrible time with that great sword beating into him.'

'So that's what it was,' Jo Henry looked as if he planned murder for whoever had buckled on the sword.

Red Smith now sat up gingerly. Charlotte thought he might be going to thank her for saving him. But instead he glowered round at the assembled company. 'Do you realise if I'd been seriously hurt, you'd have had no movie star – and no movie star means no movie!' With which he lumbered upwards and hobbled off towards his caravan.

There was a worried silence.

But soon the story of Charlotte's brave action dispelled the gloom, and she was being treated as a heroine. Reggie Leopold appeared with Bert and Cheryl from the coffee van. He put his arm round her and announced proudly, 'My daughter the wild horse tamer!'

'Don't be silly, Dad,' said Charlotte, as modestly as possible. 'I was just in the right place at the right time.'

'Nonsense!' cried Reggie. 'We will now find my mate Bert at the never-stop-eats-van and pinch a bowl of sugar lumps.'

'That is a good idea!' Charlotte thought that it would be a very good idea if her father came to the film every day.

Chapter 8

LEAVING THE GREAT PARK

Reggie Leopold didn't come filming again. He said it was all very well having a film star for a daughter but he didn't fancy being part of her fan club. Not for more than a day anyway. Besides, he'd put on too much weight with all those bacon sandwiches.

He had made a difference to their visits, however. For now Cheryl and Bert were thick as thieves, chatting and giggling as if they'd been best friends all their lives. Charlotte found it rather sickening. Cheryl sat in the front now, saying it gave Charlotte space to stretch out.

At the film location all was progressing. Since his fall Red had spent more time in his caravan which seemed to make everybody jollier. Gorgeous said he was certainly 'plotting' but Miranda W.P. who had less sense of the dramatic said he was 'licking his wounds.'

Today was the last day in Windsor Great Park. Tomorrow they would pack up and move to a new location at a grand house in the country. There was an end of term feeling about the place. Everybody packed and ran and shouted without the usual head-down feeling of desperation.

Everybody, that is, except Charlotte. Today was a very special day for her. She was to speak her very first lines. 'Oh, Papa,' she had to say, 'why are you lying so still? What is that red stuff on your coat? Oh, papa are you hurt?'

Charlotte liked these words very much. She wished she'd thought of them when Red had been lying on the ground in real life.

'Oh, papa,' she practised in front of the mirror, 'why are you lying so still?' She admired the way her eyes rolled upwards with daughterly concern. 'Oh, what is that red stuff on your coat?' Each word popped from her mouth so clearly, so expressively.

'Whatever are you doing?' Jo Henry's loud voice cut into her performance.

'Rehearsing my lines,' replied Charlotte self-righteously.

'Well, don't.'

'What?' Charlotte looked at him with surprise.

'It's perfectly dreadful. What you're doing. Like Greta Garbo out of Dallas. Just come out and do what I tell you. That's all I want.'

'Oh,' Charlotte's face crumpled. Horrid tears began behind her eyes.

Jo Henry stopped on his way out. 'That's better. That's more like it.'

'What?' Charlotte was confused.

'Now you look really upset.'

'But I'm not acting now.'

'Quite.' Jo Henry looked at her.

Charlotte thought for a bit. 'I see. You want me not to act being upset.'

'That's right.'

'But how can I seem upset if I'm not?'

'You'll have to work that out. If you do what I tell you, that'll be a start.' He turned and left the caravan.

Charlotte followed him slowly. Jo Henry's temper had become very short lately. She felt very nervous indeed.

Red Smith lay on the ground groaning. Charlotte ran to him. She crouched down. 'Oh, papa, why are you lying so still?' Suddenly the image of her own father came into her mind. What if he was hurt one day when he was far away on his tanker. Tears started in her eyes. 'What is that red stuff on your coat?' She leant over him closer. What if her father died! All alone. 'Oh, papa, are you hurt?' She felt her face go stiff and cold with terror.

'CUT and print!'

Charlotte looked up, dazed. Jo Henry was walking towards her. Red Smith sat up and rubbed the side he'd been lying on.

Jo Henry took Charlotte's hands. 'That was very good,' he said solemnly. 'No acting at all.'

'First I was Elizabeth. And then I thought of my father,' said Charlotte.

'Ah.' Jo Henry nodded wisely.

'But can she do it again?' Red Smith's drawling, mocking voice grated on Charlotte's ears.

'Of course,' Charlotte gave him a dignified look. For she knew she could find that well of sadness whenever she imagined her beloved father ill and alone on the high seas.

'That's my girl!' Jo Henry gave her a hug. He called out, 'Let's go for another take as soon as possible.'

In fact they only tried twice more before Jo Henry was happy. He, too, seemed affected by the move to a new location. He was as energetic as usual but not in the same ringmaster, bullying way. It was as if his mind was elsewhere.

Ruby eased Charlotte out of her dress and said, 'Going to the film show, tonight, are you?'

Charlotte didn't understand. 'I don't know. What is it?'

'They're showing the film they've shot so far. The old monster Bernard B. Bagelman's bringing the big American backers.'

'Oh,' said Charlotte, still not really understanding. 'But I thought it was all in bits. Like a puzzle. You can't put a puzzle together until you've got all the bits.'

'They're showing the bits.'

'I see.' Charlotte stepped into her dress which Ruby held out for her. She would miss being waited on when the film finished. 'No-one's asked me to come so I suppose I'm not.'

'It's probably after your bed-time,' Ruby said in a jolly consoling voice.

This put Charlotte on her mettle. Why shouldn't she see the bits? She was a part of the film as much as anyone. She marched along to Jo Henry's caravan. Before she knocked she reminded herself how pleased he'd been with her lines.

'Enter!'

'It's me, Charlotte.'

'Come in, then.'

Charlotte hesitated. She hardly recognised him. He wore a pale blue and white striped suit, a white shirt, white shoes and, most astonishingly of all, a pale blue tie. 'You look beautiful,' she breathed.

He nodded, impatiently. 'Got a problem, have you?'

Charlotte now realised that she had passed several other members of the film crew dressed in unusually elegant clothes. Gorgeous too had been wearing a suit though his was all white which showed off his now completely rainbow hair very nicely. Red Smith had worn a tall cowboy's hat and cream suede jacket. This film showing was obviously going to be some sort of party. It made her all the more determined not to miss it.

'I want to come and see the bits?'

'Bits? What bits?'

Charlotte saw Jo Henry was back to his ill humour again. He seemed very nervous, in fact, rubbing his hands together and biting the inside of his mouth.

'The film showing.'

'Ha. Ha.' He laughed without mirth and stood up. 'So

you want to join the gang, do you? Film showing. Ha. Two weeks rushes. Ridiculous. Not that I'm ashamed. What we've got is terrific. Terrific! Sensational!'

At this point Charlotte saw he was talking to himself, trying to calm his fears so she kept very quiet.

Jo Henry began to march up and down the little caravan. 'It's a rotten idea. Bagelman and Red Smith showing their power over me, that's what it is. Proving they're running the ship, not me. Well, we'll see. I've got a bit of life in me yet.' As he turned he suddenly noticed Charlotte again.

'So you want to come too?'

'Yes, please,' said Charlotte patiently.

Jo Henry gave a bleak guffaw. 'Everyone else is. That's the only way I could get my own back. No sneaky private showing with me crushed between the biggies like a little minnow. No. No. We'll have the whole lot there. Uncle Tom Cobbley and all.' He stopped and gave Charlotte a serious look. 'Of course, you can come. Perhaps you'll charm the American money and keep us all in business.'

The film showing was in a part of London Charlotte had never visited. The streets were very narrow with lots of little alleyways and red-lit doors. Bert who was driving, nudged Cheryl, 'They can show you a thing or two round here.'

'Sshh.' Cheryl glanced back at Charlotte.

Charlotte had two worries. Firstly she was not wearing a new or pretty dress. In fact it had been worn by Iris, Pansy and Marigold before her. Secondly, she didn't know what Jo Henry meant by 'charming American money'. But whatever it meant she didn't feel she'd be able to do it in her old dress.

Bert stopped the car. 'All change!' he winked at Cheryl. 'Just down to your suspenders, dear.'

Charlotte saw Ruby standing in front of some glass doors. Ruby would help her. She jumped out of the car.

Ruby said, 'So you buzzing-well made it, after all – excuse my Mexican.'

Ruby escorted Charlotte up some stairs. Cheryl had decided to keep Bert company since he had not been invited to the showing.

Charlotte paraded upwards. Ruby had wound a beautiful multi-coloured shawl round her shoulders. She felt like a film star. Because she was small, the silken tassels with which it was trimmed brushed against her legs every time she took a step.

'What is American money?' she asked Ruby and explained Jo Henry's remark.

'That would be the chap this is all laid on for. Howard S. Schute.'

The cinema was very small. Instead of rows of seats it had large padded swivel chairs and at the back some huge leather armchairs. Besides, it was a small room filled with a lot of very big people, most smoking cigarettes and some smoking cigars. The atmosphere was so smoky that Charlotte could hardly recognise anyone. She clung to Ruby's hand.

'Do you want an orange juice, duckie?'

'Yes, please.' Her voice had become very small.

The orange juice was in a glass with a tall stem and so filled with ice that she couldn't find any liquid to drink. Whenever she tried a hard block of ice fell forward and hit her on the nose.

'If it isn't my little Elizabeth!' A booming voice which she had heard once before made her look up. First she saw a long cigar and then she saw the large red face of the man who had sat behind the desk when she had been chosen for the film, Bernard B. Bagelman.

'So how do you like the real thing?' As he spoke an inch-long section of ash which had been attached to the end of his cigar, fell downwards. Charlotte watched as it fell directly into her glass. It puffed up a little and then lay in a thick layer over the top.

65

She looked back up to Mr Bagelman. But to her surprise, he didn't seem to have noticed. In fact he now turned his back on her and began talking to Red Smith who was noticeable because he was still wearing his cowboy hat.

Charlotte looked down again. It really was disgusting. In fact it made her feel quite sick.

'Don't tell me you English girls drink beer?'

A man had crouched down in front of her. He had a brown face with very large glasses and a very friendly smile. It was particularly nice to see someone at her own level.

'It's not beer,' she explained. 'It's a cigar.'

'Smoking, too,' he said, giving her a little nudge so she should know he was joking.

Charlotte tried to smile back but didn't really succeed. 'It's Bernard B. Bagelman's cigar ash. It fell into my orange. And now I don't know what to do.'

'Well, don't drink it for sure!'

Charlotte felt herself turn a shade paler. The American, she had recognised his accent now, took her arm. 'Come on now. Hand it to me and you'll be chirpy as a chaffinch!'

'It's being so small,' explained Charlotte who felt much better the moment he removed the glass. 'I can't get to the air.'

'I'm small too.' He stood up and put the glass on a table.

'So you are.' He barely came up to Red Smith's shoulders who was standing with his back to them.

'And I've finished growing.' He gave his nice friendly grin so Charlotte could see he wasn't too worried. 'But do you know why I don't mind?'

'No.'

He bent down again and whispered into Charlotte's ear, 'Because I've got so much money!' He looked at Charlotte delightedly. 'Have you heard the expression, "standing on your money"?'

'No,' said Charlotte meditatively. A suspicion was growing in her mind.

'Well, I stand on my money and do you know what that makes me? That makes me VERY TALL!'

'I know who you are now!' Charlotte clapped her hands excitedly, 'You're the American money!'

The man stopped. He looked at her. For a moment she thought he was cross. But then he too clapped his hands. 'So right. You are so right. That's exactly what I am and all these great big people here,' he gave a scornful look to Red and B.B.B. 'who drop cigar ash about and wear hats like steeples are terrified of me!' He turned back to Charlotte. 'So us small people must stick together. Right. And make sure we get just as much air as we need!'

Chapter 9

THE AMERICAN MONEY

Howard S. Schute or The American Money, as he now insisted on being called, took Charlotte into the cinema on his arm. He sat her down in the swivel chair next to his and held her hand throughout the entire screening.

When the lights went down he nudged her and whispered 'Excited?' to which she replied 'Very'. He held her hand firmly in a warm leathery grip of the sort few grown-ups (apart from Charlotte's father) could achieve.

When she appeared on the screen he gave an extra squeeze and then the thumbs up sign with his other hand. His cheerfulness was very different from Charlotte's neighbour on the other side. This was the author. He had not bothered to put on fancy clothes and sat so hunched over that Charlotte wondered how he could see the screen.

However by the end of the showing he had straightened up into a rigid uprightness and his groans and sighs had changed to little grunts of what might be surprised pleasure.

On Schute's other side lounged Bernard B. Bagelman. He was so big and fat that every now and again his revolving chair squeaked protestingly. At one point he got out another huge cigar but Schute gave him such a fierce look that he put it away again. Charlotte couldn't resist giving the thumbs up sign.

Jo Henry was nowhere to be seen.

Charlotte couldn't pretend she enjoyed watching the bits of film very much. For the first few minutes she enjoyed seeing all the faces she knew turned into giant technicolour on the screen. But when the same scene was repeated over and over again, sometimes from one angle and sometimes from another, she began to get very, very bored. She couldn't even enjoy watching herself pick up a piece of paper from the ground more than once. Well, twice, at the outside.

Watching herself was rather interesting and odd. Her dress was pretty, though a bit more used-looking than she'd expected. Her face seemed more babyish than it was usually, her cheeks rounder and her mouth smaller. In fact she really didn't like looking at herself either. The ringlets on the other hand, were a triumph! Every curl so smooth and shiny. She would concentrate on them.

After what seemed a very long time indeed, the lights went up again. Charlotte waited for the usual buzz and chatter. But, apart from a bit of stretching and coughing, there was total silence. She looked round. Everybody seemed to be waiting for something.

Then Bernard B. Bagelman heaved himself towards the American Money. His poor chair squeaked miserably. 'So, what do you think, Howard?'

The silence became even more intense. Charlotte noticed the writer had returned to his hunched position. And that Jo Henry was standing at the side with his arms crossed and an angry look on his face.

'Well, Bernie,' Schute gave Charlotte's hand a final squeeze and let go of it, 'so you want to know what I think first of all?'

'Objective eye, y'know.' Bagelman got out his cigar again and waved it in the air.

'With all these experts here, that makes me nervous. That makes me very nervous.' He smiled round at the film crew. 'I wouldn't ask them how to make money, now would I?'

'Ha! Ha!' Bagelman laughed loudly as if Schute had made a very good joke.

Everybody else laughed, though less loudly, and stopped and waited again.

'I'll tell you what?' Schute continued to smile. 'Why don't we find out what the experts feel first?'

'Ah. Er. Guh!' Bagelman's face fought against an expression of rage.

'What do you think, for instance?'

'Me? Ah. Grrh.'

Charlotte had never seen anyone look as silly as Bagelman did. Eyes popping, mouth twisting. He seemed either incapable or terrified of giving an opinion.

'You don't have a view then?' continued the American Money. He turned to Charlotte. 'What do you think about that, the producer has no view of his own film? What about you, then. I expect you've got something to say?' He looked at her enquiringly.

Charlotte did have something to say. Something very sensible. But at that moment she was struck with a desire to sneeze. This made her unable to speak. She half opened her mouth. The whole cinema waited expectantly. The sneeze would not come. She half closed her eyes in agony. It was coming. Nearly there. Schute's eyes behind their large glasses watched her with some surprise.

'Atishoo! Atishoo! Atishoo!' At last. The noise exploded in her ears. What a relief! She settled her face down again and smiled at the American Money who had retreated into his seat. 'What I think is you should ask Jo Henry. After all he is the director. And he does care so much, it's a labour of love, you see. Like, er, *The Blood Bandit*. At least something

71

like that . . . Anyway he knows exactly what he's doing which no-one else does as far as I can see . . .'

She was interrupted by a second explosion coming from behind her. This time it was not a sneeze but rage. Red Smith had turned the colour of his name and appeared to be tearing his hat in half. He had only just removed it from his head, thus revealing poor Gorgeous who had barely caught a glimpse of the screen.

'It's ridiculous!' Red shouted, 'Asking a child . . . call him a director . . . who knows what he's up to? . . . more like a secret agent . . .'

'Ah,' said Schute politely, 'so you agree with the young lady. I should ask Jo here what he's up to?'

'Ask him . . . ask him . . . I tell you it's like getting nuclear secrets from the Kremlin.'

'Ha,' said Schute, 'Very witty.' To Charlotte's surprise he then stood up and said calmly, 'so that's settled then. I'll arrange a meeting with Jo for tomorrow.' He turned to the gently popping face of Bernard B. Bagelman. 'Thank you Bernie. I'll have my car now. I have an appointment back at the hotel. A very useful evening, I think.'

So that was that. No-one had said what they thought about the film.

On reflection Charlotte decided that was the most sensible reaction. For, after all, how could you judge a few bits from an unfinished puzzle? On the other hand, she could see that in some way she couldn't quite understand it had been a defeat for Red Smith and Bernard B. Bagelman and a victory for Jo Henry. And that made her happy – even if he did shout at everybody.

There was no filming the day after the showing and for once Charlotte was glad to do absolutely nothing. But the following day a whole new excitement began. Since the house they were using was a two-hour drive from London, Charlotte was to stay in a hotel. She had never stayed in a hotel before.

Lily didn't like the idea at all. 'My poor little girl, all on her own in a great big echoing room.'

'There is Cheryl,' Reggie pointed out.

'She doesn't go to bed at the same time,' Lily could be very firm when she believed in something. 'What she needs is another child.'

So when they set off in Bert's car at their usual early hour of the morning, Iris sat beside Charlotte.

The choice of Iris had caused much argument among the sisters. If she had been merely going as a companion, Marigold and Pansy would have seen that, as the eldest, she had first rights. But she was also to act as an extra in a crowd scene. And everybody knew Iris hated acting. Iris was a shy, retiring sort of girl, tall and thin, who was happiest lying alone on her bed reading a book. She hated dressing-up and she hated being looked at by anyone let alone a whole crowd of people.

Iris, Pansy and Marigold agreed, was quite the wrong person to go into films. So, in fact, did Iris who, on top of everything else tended to be car-sick. But that left Lily to decide between Pansy and Marigold. And this, it soon became clear, was impossible.

'I'm older!'

'I'm a better actor!'

'You call wiggling your stomach acting?' (Pansy had acted a belly dancer in the school play).

'You've got a lisp!'

'You've got a spot.'

'You're fat!'

'You're ugly!'

So in the end, Lily really had to choose Iris. Poor Iris. She sat in the car looking very pale and nervous. Lily had given her a plastic bag to be sick into in case they were on the motorway and Bert couldn't stop in time. No-one doubted she would be sick at some point.

Charlotte held her cold hand and thought how lucky she was to have such a kind and unselfish sister. She gave her a big smile. Iris smiled back wanly.

To everybody's amazement Iris still had not been sick three hours later. The car turned into a long driveway and stopped in front of a grand house.

Cheryl leant over the front seat, 'Congratulations!' she cried.

Iris gave her an anguished look and scrambled out of the car. She stared at the elegant golden gravelled driveway, gulped and bent low.

'Well!' Bert shook his head.

'After we'd stopped,' grimaced Cheryl.

'She often does that,' explained Charlotte, 'she says it's the relief of arriving. It makes her feel all funny.'

Charlotte looked up in awe. They were standing in a huge hall. You could have fitted into it four houses the size of the Leopolds' – including their roofs. The walls were decorated by rows of stuffed animals' heads. Their glass eyes glinted in the semi-darkness. She recognised lions, tigers, fishes, deer and a crocodile complete with tail. There was also something large and hairy she thought might be a bison and something else with a particularly nasty expression that she couldn't recognise at all.

'What's that?' she asked Cheryl. 'It reminds me of something.'

Cheryl didn't answer, but Iris peered helpfully in her short-sighted way. 'I know who it looks like.'

And at the same moment so did Charlotte. 'Bernard B. Bagelman!' They shrieked together. And were off again, laughing like hyaenas.

Miranda arrived a second later and demanded to know the joke. She looked at the stuffed head and she looked at the girls. 'You're absolutely right,' she said. 'It's the spitting image.' She grabbed an electrician who was passing with a

great coil of flex. 'Seen Jo Henry's beheaded our producer?' She pointed at the wall.

The electrician doubled up with laughter and grabbed Gorgeous who'd come to find the girls. 'There's Bernie B.B. with glass eyes!'

Gorgeous went, 'Ooh, my word, what a delicious sight!' and beckoned Ruby who was just descending a grand marble staircase.

Ruby laughed so much that the tassels on her table-cloth dress danced as if they were alive. She called over Digger, draped about as usual with his wires and boxes.

Soon the hall was filled with the entire film crew with the exception of Jo Henry, all falling about with laughter.

'Oh, oh,' Ruby wiped her eyes. 'What a perfectly splendid start to the day!' Gradually they peeled away back to their jobs, though with many a backward glance to the stuffed head.

'Dearie me,' Gorgeous took Charlotte's hand and led her upstairs, 'You can see our producer isn't exactly popular round here.'

'Does everyone hate him?' asked Iris as they entered a small panelled room hung about with the usual lights and jewels.

'Yes,' answered Miranda definitely.

'I used to think you hated Jo Henry too,' Charlotte said meditatively.

'Oh, we do.' Gorgeous fluffed up his rainbow-coloured hair. 'He's such a bully. And he never tells us what's going on.'

'But without him there'd never be a film. Not one worth all our flipping time and energy – excuse my Japanese.' Ruby came in and walked round Iris with a resigned expression. 'You're tall for your age, dear, aren't you? And thin.'

Iris looked apologetic. She clutched, as if for protection, the pile of books she'd brought to fill the waiting time.

'Well, I love Jo Henry!' cried Charlotte. 'I think he cares

76

about the film more than anything.'

Gorgeous opened his eyes in mock surprise. 'But we all love him! Don't we dears?' He looked round at Miranda and Ruby who nodded solemnly. 'Just because we hate him, it doesn't mean we don't love him too. Some of us have worked with him three or four times before. We hate him in a quite different way we hate the Stuffed Head.'

'Oh,' said Charlotte. She paused. 'Well, I'm glad.'

'We hate Red Smith too,' continued Gorgeous, 'and sometimes we hate Helen Wittering but that's more in the way we hate Jo Henry, poor dear.'

'And now,' said Ruby, 'we will adjourn to the costume room.' She looked at the girls' bewildered faces. 'Another week or two and you'll understand it all.'

'Oh, but I do now,' said Charlotte, 'You hate Jo Henry and Helen like I hate Fred and Ned which means I love them too. While you hate Red and Bagelman like I hate Miss Doughty at school because she really is horrible.'

'Such brilliance from one so young!' Ruby smiled and pushed her out of the room.

Chapter 10

A STATELY HOME

That morning they were filming a breakfast scene. Lady Clarissa was eating a generous portion of meat cutlets. Her husband, dressed in flowing silk, picked at a roast piglet. Charlotte had to run in the room crying out, 'Three men are galloping up the drive. They're holding swords and look very fierce.'

This proved to be very difficult to say while running. For one thing she was wearing a different dress which was longer than the other. For another the door handle was very stiff so she could never come in on cue. (The cue was a tinkling laugh from Lady Clarissa). And, worst of all, her entrance was met with such looks of fury from her supposedly loving father, that she stuttered and forgot her words.

Jo Henry who had started exceptionally calm, soon began his dancing around and wild grimacing. He spoke to Charlotte through half-closed mouth as if, if he opened it, any further screams of frustration would escape. 'Just say the lines. Just come in and say the lines. I don't care how you do it. Sing them if you like. Just look at your parents and speak.'

'Yes, Jo Henry.' Charlotte gulped and retreated for yet another try.

'Leave the door open for the little idiot!' she heard Jo Henry shout after her. 'And tell her not to speak till she's got into the room and standing still.' Digger, who was outside the door, gave Charlotte an encouraging squeeze.

'He's got a lot of worries,' he whispered.

'I hate him!'

'Aha. So now you really are part of the family.'

In fact Charlotte's hatred gave her just the energy needed to enter the room at a run, stop suddenly and cry out with a fearful expression, 'Three men are galloping up the drive. They're holding swords and looking very fierce.' She didn't even care about her silly dress any more.

'There! I knew you could do it.' Jo Henry came over and gave her a big kiss. Much to her embarrassment, Charlotte felt herself blushing. 'And since that was perfect we'll take a break there and carry on after lunch.'

Cheryl and Iris were already at the lunch. Trestle-tables had been set up in a huge old kitchen. Copper pots and pans lined the walls. Iris was very depressed. She had tried on her costume and said she looked like a broomstick. All the other girl extras who were her age had nice little bosoms to puff up their necklines and she had nothing at all. Really, it was too humiliating.

'What about rolled up socks?' suggested Cheryl. 'I had just the same problem at your age. Size 5 white cotton always worked wonders.'

'Don't worry, dearie.' Gorgeous patted her hand. 'Mine have never grown at all and look where I've got to!'

'Sshh, Gorgeous,' Ruby plonked her huge form on the bench. 'Personally, I don't believe we'll ever get to your scene this afternoon. They've still got to finish the breakfast scene and the mood Red Smith's in, that could take hours. Besides, if you look out of the window you'll see large rain clouds. By tomorrow I'll find you a better costume.'

'I wonder,' Iris hesitated shyly, 'I wonder if I could possibly be a boy?'

'A boy. Of course you can. That's a wizard idea. I'm short of pages. There, I knew we'd sort it out.'

They all settled down to lamb cutlets, which were very nice, although Charlotte was disappointed to see no baby piglet.

Red Smith no longer ate with the rest of the cast. Charlotte saw his dresser collect him six lamb cutlets and a mound of cheese.

'Red's on a high protein diet,' she explained to Iris. Everybody knew about Red's diets. He never stayed on one more than a few days but it made him very demanding. The worst had been the drinking man's diet when he'd consumed huge quantities of neat whiskey. His voice had become even more slurred than usual and he walked with a strange lop-sided swing.

It had been during his whiskey diet that the horse had run away with him. He had never referred to the incident since and Charlotte thought all that drink might have made him forget all about it. Certainly it had not made him any nicer to her.

Five minutes after the dresser had taken off one out-sized portion of protein, he returned for another. Gorgeous nudged Charlotte. 'That'll be for the Stuffed Head. They're having another of their pow-wows.'

Ruby shook her head so her plump cheeks wobbled. 'That bodes no good.'

They both turned to look at Jo Henry, who was eating all on his own. As they watched, he clapped his hands above his plate. A wriggling black fly dropped onto his food. He pushed it aside with disgust.

'If only Bernard B. Bagelman was a fly,' sighed Gorgeous.

'But what about the American Money?' asked Charlotte, 'They can't do anything against his wishes.'

'He goes back to the U.S. of A. tonight.'

'The night of the long swords,' Miranda jabbed out her arm as if she held a sword.

'They won't kill him?' Iris asked with round frightened eyes.

'Being chucked off your own picture is worse than death for a director,' said Gorgeous solemnly.

They all sat with glum faces. Until Digger appeared and shouted, 'What in snowball's sake are you doing sitting around when we're supposed to be shooting in five minutes!'

'Shooting?' shivered Iris with her mind still on murder. So Charlotte explained and they all dashed away to prepare for the breakfast scene once more.

Red Smith had made Helen Wittering cry. She sat on the other side of the grand breakfast table with tears streaming down her face. He had told her she was as little like a star as the woman who came and did his laundry. He drawled, 'Why don't you go back to the kitchen sink and stop pretending to be something you're not.'

Charlotte stared, horrified. She had never seen a grown-up cry so much. The water had brought her eye make-up flooding down her cheeks so that she looked like a Red Indian before a war dance.

Jo Henry was keeping surprisingly calm. He beckoned Red into a corner. Charlotte noticed Jo Henry was looking particularly small. Usually he was so loud and energetic that he seemed to fill a lot of space. Now he was quiet and small. She could only hear Red's voice.

'I'm going to make it impossible for you . . . you'll go long before that . . . you care more about the picture than yourself, right? . . . I'm a winner . . . without me, this picture doesn't exist . . . I could buy up the whole lot of you . . . .'

Miranda was studying Helen's face. 'It's no good,' she said, 'I'll have to take you upstairs. Ice-cubes, face pack, head between your knees. The lot.' This started Helen crying all over again and Miranda led her away.

Charlotte sat down on one of the dining-room chairs. No-one took any notice of her. She wondered if she dared go and find Cheryl and Iris, who were not allowed on the set.

'You're a minnow! Right. A minnow!' Red's voice came even louder from the corner. Then his boots came clumping along the wooden floor. He swept past Charlotte and out of the door.

'Early tea break!' called Digger with an unusual air of desperation in his voice.

Outside the large bow window, it began to rain. Charlotte saw a slight figure come running from the trees towards the house. As he came nearer, she recognised the writer's pale and miserable face.

'Well, at least I didn't hit the great animal.' Charlotte turned to Jo Henry's voice. He had sat down beside her. Everybody else had left the room. 'Or perhaps I should have hit him. At least I'd feel happier.' He began to bite at his fingers.

Charlotte tried to think of something comforting. 'Have a piece of toast?' She slid over the silver toast-rack.

'Don't. That's how it started. He wouldn't spoil his protein diet by eating toast.'

'How silly!'

'Quite.' Jo Henry gave her a little smile. 'Of course, he's just looking for any old excuse to make things difficult. Impossible. He wants me off the picture.'

'Why?'

'Ha. Ha. There's a question. Because he doesn't like me. Because I don't like him. Because he wants a director he can direct. Because he's a loathsome worm.'

Now Charlotte smiled. 'A very big and fat and hairy worm. Ugh.'

'Ugh, indeed,' agreed Jo Henry. 'But he wants me to resign. If they chuck me off they'll have to pay me.'

'That's all right, then.' Charlotte felt brighter. 'You just

82

don't go.'

Jo Henry stood up and went to the window. The rain battered crossly at the glass. 'If I don't go, they'll make sure the film is wrecked. Bagelman won't want that but he can't control Red Smith. And it's just another film to him. He'll get his money either way. He hates me now.' Jo Henry ran

his finger along the window pane. 'If I go at least the film will be made. It took me two years to get it started you know. I paid for the script myself. I only sold out to Bagelman at the end. But I can't let it all go to waste.' He looked round the room. 'All this. All you people. The crew. I can't let it all be for nothing.'

Charlotte felt very sad. Jo Henry looked as unhappy as a grown-up can without crying. She couldn't imagine he would ever actually cry. She certainly hoped not.

There was a long pause. Charlotte began to feel restless. She drummed her feet softly against the chair. Eventually she stood up. 'I think I should find my sister.'

But Jo Henry didn't reply. He stood by the window staring out at the rain. Charlotte tiptoed quietly out and then ran all the way upstairs.

It rained heavily all afternoon. Charlotte wasn't called again so she and Iris played dominoes. The house seemed unusually silent as if there'd been a death as Iris put it, shuddering.

They were relieved when Digger told them they could go to their hotel. He didn't know yet what time they'd be wanted in the morning.

Chapter 11

RED SMITH LOSES HIS WIG

The hotel was disappointing from the outside. It stood on a wide busy road, it was square, it was built of grey concrete, now streaked with rain. But inside presented a much more cheerful scene. Soft lights glowed from every corner, a red carpet bounced luxuriously under their feet and dark-suited men rushed about to do their bidding.

It turned out they were the first of the film company to arrive. Charlotte and Iris felt very grand and Charlotte said, 'Yes, I am a film actress, and play the leading lady's daughter.' This provoked endless admiration and comments about her youth.

'I suppose you've been in films since you were a baby?' asked one of the admiring circle.

This was a little awkward. Charlotte glanced at Cheryl. No. She could not lie. 'Actually, this is my first film.'

'Your first film. Well, I never. And you so calm.'

'I have been in it for several weeks,' said Charlotte, feeling her pride somewhat restored.

'And your sister. Is she in it too?'

'I'm just an extra,' Iris looked longingly up the stairs.

'Just an extra! Well I never. What a talented pair.'

In the end they were quite glad to escape up to their bedroom. The wonderful carpeting was there too. Iris sank to the floor and ran her fingers over the soft pile. 'It must have cost a fortune.'

'It's everywhere,' agreed Charlotte, 'even up the walls of the lift.'

'You hardly need beds,' said Iris as Charlotte sank down beside her on the floor.

The day had been eventful. They had risen early. In a matter of seconds their eyes had closed and they were both fast asleep.

Cheryl, who had been drinking with Bert in the bar, found them an hour later. 'Well, honestly. With all the lovely facilities, to use the floor!' She shook Iris and then Charlotte.

'Where am I?' They woke up quite scared.

'On the floor.'

Charlotte and Iris looked round. So they were. They staggered up and, hardly bothering to open their eyes, made for the twin beds.

'You've got to undress!' cried Cheryl as they threw themselves down.

The result of this unseemly behaviour was that the two girls woke up very early the next morning wearing only their knickers. Clear, dawn light poured in through the windows.

After a few seconds they realised where they were. 'Cheryl might have drawn the curtains,' grumbled Charlotte.

'At least it's not raining,' Iris sat up and looked round with an excited gleam in her eyes, 'And we're in a hotel. On our own.'

'A three star hotel.' Charlotte also sat up.

'And we haven't explored at all!' Iris swung her legs out of bed. So did Charlotte.

In a moment the two girls were racing round the room. 'Our own phone!' 'Our own desk. Look at the writing paper.' 'And pen!' 'A menu. Room service. Oh, we can order breakfast up here!' 'A cupboard with a thousand hangers!' 'And a bathroom. All to ourselves. No Ned, Fred, Pansy, Marigold to mess it all up. I've never seen anywhere so clean and shiny!'

Iris sat on the closed lavatory and Charlotte sat on the edge of the bath. They grinned at each other. They could see their faces repeated in glittering mirrors all round the walls.

'This is just like being in a book,' sighed Iris.

Charlotte looked upwards. 'Shall we have a shower or a bath?'

'Or both?' suggested Iris.

Half an hour later they both returned to their beds looking exceptionally clean. 'Now I really do feel like someone out of a film,' said Iris. She picked up the telephone. 'Do you think it's too early to order breakfast?'

'I don't know what time it is.'

'Neither do I.'

'What number please?' An efficient voice came over the telephone. Without thinking Iris gave their home number. In a moment they heard their father's voice repeating the number.

'It's me, Iris!'

Charlotte hopped over to join her. 'And me, too,' she cried excitedly.

'Whatever time is it?' Reggie's voice sounded blurred with sleep.

'We don't know. It's wonderful here. The carpet's like a bed and we've had a shower and a bath and we're about to order bacon and scrambled eggs followed by orange juice and porridge and half a grapefruit . . .'

'It's 6 o'clock,' said Reggie. He did not sound very pleased.

'Oh,' Iris screwed up her eyes. 'That is early.'

'Yes. Still, now you've woken me. How's the filming?'

'Terribly dramatic. Everybody's fighting. And crying.'

'It sounds just like home life,' Reggie laughed. 'Mum wants to know if you're well. You sound a bit *too* well if you ask me.'

'Do you think we can order breakfast yet?' shouted Charlotte.

'It depends if the bar's open for your champagne and orange juice.'

'Oh, Dad.'

'Give us a ring this evening, your mum says. Bye now.'

'Bye.'

Charlotte and Iris stared at each other. They both felt a little bit homesick, though they weren't going to admit it.

'Go on then, order breakfast.'

While they were waiting for it to arrive Charlotte went to the window. Their room overlooked the road in front of the hotel. A car was parked there with one of the film drivers standing near. As she watched two figures came out. One was Jo Henry, the other, the writer. They didn't speak to each other but got in the car with gloomy faces.

Iris joined Charlotte at the window. She too looked down. 'They start work early,' she commented.

'I don't know,' Charlotte watched the departing car doubtfully. But then there was a knock on the door and a trolley laden with food was wheeled in. So she forgot all about the hunched figures.

They were to film the crowd scene that morning. Gorgeous' make-up room was filled with new faces. Ruby had so many to costume that she had overflowed into a second room. She had kept her word and found Iris a very elegant page's costume. It had shiny knee breeches and rosettes on the shoes. Iris spun about delightedly. Her hair had been coiled into a velvet cap with a feather.

'You're quite unrecognisable!' cried Charlotte.

'I suppose that is a compliment.' Iris stopped twirling about. 'The funny thing is I don't feel shy dressed up like this. I feel as if the real me is all hidden away somewhere where no-one can hurt it.'

'Perhaps you should be an actress, too,' suggested Charlotte seriously.

'Oh, no. Even now I wouldn't like to act. Draw attention to myself. I just enjoy being in disguise.'

Charlotte remembered what Jo Henry had taught her about acting – or rather not acting. 'Acting's not about being all show-off, you know, rolling your eyes and putting on a funny voice. It's being real.' But she could see Iris didn't really understand. Or perhaps she just wasn't interested enough.

The two girls went downstairs and out into the garden. Digger was pushing people into groups. The cameraman was fussing behind him holding up his light meter. Red Smith, dressed from top to toe in amber velvet, hovered near the camera. There was no sign of Jo Henry and Helen Wittering had not yet made her appearance, although Charlotte had seen her being dressed upstairs.

Then down the driveway came Bernard Bagelman's limousine. It stopped beside the cameraman and Bagelman climbed out. He looked particularly revolting, this morning, Charlotte thought, in tweed plus-fours with a little matching hat on the top of his big red face.

He and Red Smith talked for a few minutes. Everybody watched although they pretended to be following Digger's commands. Everybody knew something had happened. Even the newcomers whispered nervously. They didn't want to be out of a job before they'd even started. Was the Stuffed Head about to pull the plugs?

He took a few determined steps forward. Followed close behind by Red and his amber velvet. Charlotte noticed that Gorgeous and Ruby and Miranda and all the inside workers had come to the door of the house. Even the cooks had come out of their van. One held a steaming pan in his hand.

'Ha, Ha! I see you all know I've got something to say,' began Bagelman in a jolly voice. 'Well, the first thing I want to say is that you're all great people. And you're doing a great job on this picture.'

'Hear. Hear!' shouted an unseen voice who received a furious look from Bagelman.

'And the second thing I want to say it that I'm one hundred per cent, I repeat, one hundred per cent, behind this picture. This picture is going to go. This picture is going to be great!' He paused and stretched his mouth into a huge crocodile-like smile. 'So that's the good news.'

Everybody became very quiet.

'The bad news is that this picture is in big trouble. It's over-spent, over-time and over the barrel.' His little eyes narrowed nastily. 'Luckily it's not too late to put this right. We have a very big star with us,' he turned to Red Smith, 'who has FAITH!' He said this very loudly as if he expected people to clap. Everybody stayed quiet. 'He is not only a very big star without whom this picture would be NOTHING!' his voice rose again, 'but also a man of many and exceptional talents and out of his FAITH and good-will he has offered to take on this picture as his own. In other words we will not only be lucky enough to have A Big Star as our main actor but also as our DIRECTOR!'

There was a silence so total that even the birds seemed to have stopped singing.

Bagelman slapped Red Smith on the back, 'Good. Good. So I've said my bit. And now on with the show!' Without waiting for any response he turned and positively scuttled back to his waiting car. In a moment it had rounded the drive and disappeared out of sight.

Charlotte felt tears pricking her eyes, 'I told Jo Henry not to resign.'

'He must have been going this morning when we saw them,' said Iris wonderingly.

'And the writer,' agreed Charlotte.

'To your marks everybody!' screamed Digger.

'Isn't it cruel,' whispered Charlotte, 'the way everybody is going on without him?' But then she was taken to the front of the crowd and Iris was pushed to the back so she could say no more.

It seemed that they were all gathered together to welcome a visit from Charles I. His carriage would roll down the driveway and then they would all wave and cry, 'God Save the King'. As he stepped out of the carriage, Charlotte had to move forward a few paces, curtsey deeply and present him with a greyhound puppy. In other words, it was a very exciting scene.

'It's a hard enough scene to get right without him,' the cameraman and Digger passed in front of Charlotte. They both looked at Red with contempt. He was circling about in a restless way. Every now and again he looked through a little spy-glass or made a frame for the scene with his hands. Behind him two other men struggled along with the camera. But every time they put it down, he frowned and shook his head.

'I'd better go and show him where it should be,' the cameraman sighed.

'If we want the film to carry on,' agreed Digger.

Charlotte had never thought about the position of the camera. It always seemed to just BE in the right place. Red Smith came to take up his position beside her. He was sweating heavily and still couldn't keep still. 'So wait till the carriage comes into shot. I want the camera absolutely stationary!'

Charlotte saw the cameraman give what her mother described as an old-fashioned look. Along the driveway Digger and several others were stationed with walkie-talkie sets. They were in contact with the carriage further up the drive.

'O.K. Let the carriage roll,' shouted Red.

Round the corner came a heavy wooden vehicle pulled by two white horses. It came so slowly that it hardly appeared to be moving.

'Tell them to get a move on!' shouted Red.

'They daren't!' Digger reported back after a conversation with his walkie-talkie. 'They might never stop!'

'------------ that!' shouted Red, using a naughty swearword, 'It looks ------ ridiculous!'

The carriage began to pick up speed a little.

'Faster!' screamed Red, 'This is a living King of England arriving, not a funeral cortege.'

The carriage went faster. Charlotte could hear the creaking and rumbling. The driveway sloped downhill. The horses began to trot, then canter. 'Oh, no!' thought Charlotte, 'not again.' The crowd behind her began to move nervously. The carriage was only a few yards away. It would never stop now. She could see the terrified driver on top of the carriage pulling the reins with all his might.

'Run!' A voice called out. And in a moment the welcoming party had dispersed across the lawn. Charlotte would have run too but Red had a firm grip on her hand. The carriage swept past them a mere inch away. At the window peered the pale and desperate face of King Charles I.

'------! ------! ------!' screamed Red, using a variety of naughty words.

The horses careered on till they reached the kitchen garden at the side of the house. There they stopped of their own accord and began to eat carrot tops. King Charles I descended with trembling legs.

'Time for breakfast,' called Digger without even asking Red.

When they reassembled, a new plan had been formed. The carriage should only make the last few paces towards the crowd. They would film its progress down the driveway at a different time without Crowd or King.

Charlotte stood beside Red once more. She had been

given the greyhound to hold. It was supposed to be a puppy but she had never seen such a huge dog in her life. It was strong too and kept pulling at the leash in a frightening way. She would have told someone but Red Smith was in such a bad temper that she didn't dare move or speak. 'Sshh, Archibald,' she said under her breath which was, she thought, a very silly name for a dog.

'Quiet!' Red glared down at her. 'We're about to go.' He looked at the camera-man who gave the thumbs up sign. 'Action!'

The clapper-boy ran in and banged the boards together. And that was all Charlotte knew. Archibald, being a wily kind of greyhound, did not run forward, which Charlotte was prepared for, but whisked round and dashed backwards. Into the crowd. Once more they dispersed across the lawn. Once more Red stood alone swearing not very softly.

But this time poor Charlotte was dragged away, hanging onto the leash and running as far as her legs could move.

'Let go!' shouted a voice.

Charlotte let go and fell flat on her face.

'We can't have another breakfast,' said a voice above her head. She got up slowly. Iris came rushing to her.

'Are you all right?'

'Just out of breath.' She looked down. 'And rather dirty.' Ruby appeared, her face anguished.

'Rotting grass stains! Excuse my Dutch. Didn't I warn you about grass stains!'

Red's furious tones carried above everything, 'Get that ------ child and that ------ dog back here AT ONCE!'

'I don't think he should swear like that,' said Iris in a shocked voice.

'It's because he's out of control, dearie,' said Ruby, 'People always swear when they can't cope.' She led Charlotte back. 'Her dress is dirty,' she informed Red.

'------ that!'

So they began again. But this time one of the extras held onto the dog till the last minute and then brought it round to Charlotte. The coach stopped. A page opened the door. A cheer went up, 'God Save Our King!' King Charles I put out an elegantly-stockinged leg and hurtled head first out of the carriage. Polite cheering changed into shrieks of laughter. King Charles I got up and hopped around holding his leg. The page had forgotten to put the steps down.

'Fire him!' screamed Red.

'I suppose we could have a lunch break,' murmured a voice doubtfully.

In the face of Red's rage the laughter died down. In the pause while King Charles was given first aid the soundman approached. 'Some of the crowd,' he said to Red, 'were shouting "God Save Our Queen!"'

'Some of you were shouting "God Save Our Queen!"' screamed Red. 'Now this may be your idea of a joke but it is

not mine. What I want you to do is raise your hats in the air and cry, "God Save Our King!" King. King. KING!' Suiting action to words, he raised his own hat and waved it above his head.

A stunned silence followed. He had torn not only his hat off his head but also his hair. Underneath his seventeenth-century wig he was almost entirely bald. But Red Smith was famous for his thatch of golden hair. Worse still as he waved the hat in the air, the wig separated from it and fell onto the ground behind him. He returned the hat to his head without it. 'Let's go! he screamed and 'Let's get it right!'

No-one said anything about his lack of hair although there were a few stifled giggles and when Charlotte next looked the wig had mysteriously vanished.

So the scene began again. The carriage rolled forward. The cheers arose with heavy emphasis on the word King. King Charles I descended graciously and Charlotte and

Red stepped forward. The King held out his jewelled hand. This was the signal for Red to take off his hat and sweep a low bow, and Archibald to be led forward to Charlotte. It should have been a most charming and elegant scene.

What happened was that Red made his low bow and found himself face to face with his wig. In the jaws of the greyhound. He gave a kind of groan and put his hand to his naked head. The groan grew to a moan. All around him was silent. The moment was awful in its pleasure.

Red snatched forward for the wig. The dog crouched away. He saw this man wanted to play. Red snatched again. Archibald bounced sideways. He shook the wig between his teeth. His tail wagged invitingly. Red lunged. Missed. The dog ran a few paces. Red followed. The dog ran further. So did Red.

Round the carriage. Back again. Towards the lawn. The crowd parted helpfully. Across the lawn. Round and round the lawn. The excited happy greyhound bounding along. The bald furious man dressed in amber velvet stumbling behind. At first he had breath to shout, 'I'll kill him! I'll kill you all!' But after a while he ran silently.

Now and again Archibald got so far ahead that he turned and stopped, waiting, eyes bright, till Red got closer. Once he even laid down the wig and let Red get right up to it before he snatched it away.

Red's humiliation was so perfect, so complete that even those who disliked him most began to feel pity after a while. Ruby picked up his hat and took it towards him. The crowd closed in and cornered the dog. The wig was retrieved. Without a word Red Smith walked into the house.

The cameraman and Digger stood beside Charlotte. 'We could never have used the scene anyway.'

'Why not?'

'No Lady Clarissa.'

'You're quite right. And he never even noticed.' A pause. 'Did you get it all on film?'

'Yes.'

'All? All of it? To the end?'

'Every last bald inch.' They laughed together briefly and then the cameraman gave a crafty smile. 'I'll personally make sure it's printed.'

Digger smiled too. 'That would be sensible.'

Red Smith did not appear again that day. The cameraman, who Charlotte now discovered was called Julie – rather odd for a man, she thought – directed instead. It was a simple scene in which Charlotte walked through the garden with her mother and they got on rather well.

Charlotte said to Helen Wittering: 'Why weren't you here this morning?'

Helen gave her a blank look, 'Ask no questions and you'll get no lies.'

Charlotte persisted, 'Was it because you didn't want to be directed by Red Smith?'

'Curiosity killed the cat!' Helen turned away but not before giving such a huge wink that Charlotte knew she'd been right.

'Well, I think none of us should work for him!' she cried.

Helen looked over her shoulder, 'We're not, are we?'

Charlotte caught Julie's eye, 'I think Jo Henry should be brought back!' But her defiant cry was only met by a sigh. 'Let's see what tomorrow brings.'

The next morning everybody was given a late call. They stood in the foyer of the hall waiting for their cars to arrive.

'Look at the way they're standing in groups. All huddled together and whispering,' Charlotte said to Iris.

'Something dreadful's going to happen. It's just like in films,' said Iris.

'We are in films, silly,' pointed out Charlotte.

'Sssh, girls.' Cheryl was the only one who had stayed faithful to Red Smith. 'Big stars have to be different from other people,' she had said.

'Nastier,' suggested Charlotte.

'Balder,' added Iris.

Red Smith cut his way through the crowds in the foyer. His car waited for him. The rest of the film company followed. Pretending not to look, they all noticed an unknown young man already seated in the back of the car.

They all followed him to the set.

That morning they were to film the continuation of the King Charles I arrival scene. His actual arrival in the coach and welcome seemed to have been temporarily abandoned. Red Smith appeared with his dresser in very close attendance. Archibald, the greyhound, was nowhere to be seen. 'He wanted him shot,' whispered an extra.

Charlotte, now wise about these things, looked for the camera. There it stood. There stood Julie. And there also stood the new young man.

Charlotte plucked Red's amber velvet sleeve, 'Who's that please?' she asked.

'Our ------ director,' snarled Red with the kind of vicious look adults very seldom give little girls.

'Jo Henry one day, you the next, followed by Julie in the afternoon and now this new man.' Charlotte gave Red an innocent smile, 'Do directors always change so much on films?'

'No.' Red crouched down so that he was on a level with Charlotte. 'But I'll tell you something for nothing Little

Miss Busybody, that there could be some more changes in this film. A lot more comings and even more *GOINGS*!'

As his white teeth clamped shut in an ugly leer, Charlotte made two decisions. Firstly she didn't want to be a big film star if that's what they were like. Secondly, she would find a way of getting Jo Henry back on the picture.

'Thank you,' she said in a polite small voice, 'that's most helpful.'

They then proceeded to act together under the directions of director number four. Each time had been different, Charlotte thought. With Jo Henry it had been exciting and tense and difficult but rewarding at the end. With Red it had been chaos. With Julie it had been like a gentle kind of rehearsal and now with this new man, it was something between all three.

For one thing he was very young and very nervous. He kept looking towards Red Smith as if expecting a sword thrust if he got things wrong. Apparently he'd never directed a real film before. Charlotte overheard him saying to Julie, 'I only read the script last night. But I couldn't say no, could I? When would I get another chance to break into the big time?'

Charlotte didn't hear the answer. This was the scene when she had to say 'You look so elegant, mama!' She remembered when Jo Henry had first asked her to say it in their house. And Ned and Fred had burst in screaming 'Elephant! Elephant!' It seemed a very long time ago.

She tried to pick out Iris among the crowd. Tonight they must have a long pow-wow to discuss a plan of action.

'Action!' called the new director in a slightly quavering voice. The clapper-boy ran in and out.

Charlotte took a small step forward, 'You look so elegant, mama!'

Helen Wittering, or rather Lady Clarissa, gave her a cold look, 'Do not think I do it in honour of this King your father entertains.'

'I beg your pardon, mama.' Charlotte gave a little curtsey and let her mother pass.

'Cut!' shouted the new director, gaining volume. 'And print.'

'New set-up!' called Digger.

Charlotte thought this a little odd as Helen had tripped on her dress as she moved forward. However it was not her business. She looked at Helen meditatively. She had refused to be directed by Red. That was hopeful. On the other hand she had clearly agreed to work with the new director. Less hopeful.

She and Iris would have to draw up a list of those who might help them get Jo Henry back. And those who wouldn't. Cheryl, with her adoration of Red, was obviously top of this second list. So she mustn't know anything about their plan. Which shouldn't be too difficult as she spent more and more time with Bert and less and less with the girls.

Charlotte and Iris lay in their luxurious hotel beds. It was dark. It was late. They had been plotting for hours. Now they had come to a decision. 'So we approach Gorgeous, Ruby, Miranda and Helen first. Julie, and Digger next. And then I send a telegram to The American Money.'

This was the real brain-wave of the evening. Charlotte could still imagine Schute's sympathetic face. She had no doubt if he only knew what was going on he'd come rushing back and sort it out.

He'd seen the bits of film Jo Henry had shot, and knew how good they were. He also understood the sheer awfulness of Bagelman and Red Smith.

'That leaves us with only two problems. What to actually write. What words I mean. And how to send a telegram to America?'

'And money,' murmured Iris in a very sleepy voice.

'Money,' repeated Charlotte. But she too was feeling

extremely tired. 'Money. Money.' Her voice died away and she was fast asleep.

Everybody was very edgy on the film set. Gorgeous tugged at Charlotte's ringlets and when she winced said 'Sorry, I'm sure' in an unconvincing voice. Charlotte wanted to ask him how to write to Schute but couldn't find a good moment.

Miranda brushed pink on Charlotte's cheeks and said, 'An early night for you my girl. You look like something the cat brought in.'

Ruby had been even worse, actually managing to stick a needle into Charlotte as she sewed up the back of her dress, and then saying 'Acupuncture, dearie,' in an unsympathetic voice. It was an elaborate ball gown which she had been much looking forward to wearing but now everything was spoilt. The new young director was so jittery and Red Smith so bad-tempered that it would be a miracle if anything got shot at all. Particularly the very complicated ball scene that was planned.

'I don't know how I'm expected to dress twenty heads of hair in two hours,' grumbled Gorgeous. 'They'll just have to appear in a mess that's all.'

'And what about sewing twenty apologies for human beings into their ball dresses!' Ruby put her face round the door.

'He can't just spring a scene like this on us,' Miranda dusted pink powder on Helen's shoulders so energetically that it flew round the room and made them sneeze.

Helen recovered first. 'However fierce Jo Henry was, at least he wanted the best from us all.'

'And knew how to get it,' added Gorgeous giving a vicious pull to Red Smith's wig. Red Smith, himself, no longer left his own dressing-room so the wig was carried through ready prepared.

'This new young chap thinks he's directing a corn-flakes commercial.'

'We'll be singing "Put some golden sunshine in" by the end of two weeks.'

'If he can keep going that long.'

Charlotte realised this was her moment. 'I think we should get Jo Henry back,' she said in a loud voice.

Everybody stopped working to look at her. 'How, sweetie?' Gorgeous smiled but she could see he wasn't taking her seriously.

'It's quite easy, really,' Charlotte came and stood by the make-up lights.

'Quite easy. Listen to her,' Miranda waved her powder puff again so they all sneezed again.

This time Charlotte recovered first. 'Yes, very easy. I write or send a telegram to the American Money. And tell him what's going on. Then he comes and sees how bad all the new bits are and gets back Jo Henry.' She looked round but since no-one said anything, she continued, 'My only problem is how to send the letter or telegram. That's where I need help.'

'The American Money.' Gorgeous put down his brush thoughtfully. 'I presume you mean Mr Schute?'

'Yes,' agreed Charlotte.

'Who liked you so much at the film showing,' said Miranda and to everyone's relief she tucked the powder puff away in its box.

'And who disliked Red Smith and Bagelman,' Ruby hung three dresses she was carrying on the back of the door and sat down.

Helen studied her face very close in the mirror as actresses feel compelled to do and then leant back in her chair. 'It's worth trying,' she said solemnly.

Charlotte felt a warm excitement fill her. She realised she had been holding her breath with tension. 'I knew you'd help. I knew you would.'

'We risk being fired,' said Gorgeous seriously.

'Bagelman wouldn't dare. Not at this stage of the picture.'

'He couldn't fire me,' said Helen, 'It would be too expensive to film Lady Clarissa's part all over again. And I would refuse to work if he fired you. We should get Julie and Digger and the rest of the crew to support us.'

'Bagelman will never employ us again,' said Miranda.

'That's true,' agreed Helen.

They all looked gloomy. Then Gorgeous smiled bravely, 'He's an old has-been anyway! He only got this picture going because Jo Henry had done all the work. He just happened to meet Schute at the right moment and get the money needed.'

'I wouldn't ever want to work with Bagelman again!' cried Charlotte in rallying tones.

'Hear! Hear!' agreed the others, though slightly less enthusiastically. There weren't that many jobs going in the film industry.

'So what we want to do is get in touch with Schute as quickly as possible,' said Helen.

'Or the film will be finished before he arrives.'

'Oh, we can slow things down a bit,' Gorgeous smiled grimly.

'Poor young director,' Ruby laughed without pity, 'He'll wish he never left the cereal bowl.'

'Black-leg,' growled Miranda.

'I have done a rough of the telegram,' announced Charlotte who thought they were getting off the point. 'Shall I read it?' She produced a piece of hotel writing-paper from her pocket.

'Action!' cried Gorgeous.

'Dear American Money,' began Charlotte.

'You don't say 'dear' in a telegram,' interrupted Miranda.

'Sshh,' Helen gave her a severe look. 'Let's get the gist of it first.'

'Dear American Money I know you would want me to tell you that Jo Henry isn't directing the film any more and Red Smith tried but it didn't work so now he has this young man who shakes with terror and doesn't notice when Helen trips on her dress so it's sure to be a terrible mess and that's a great pity when we've all tried so hard and particularly Jo Henry whose idea it was in the first place, it being a labour of love. He should come back, I think. So I'd be very grateful if you'd come back yourself first and put things right. From your admiring (and small) friend Charlotte (Elizabeth in the film). P.S. Bagelman seems to be staying out of it now which is good news on the horrible cigar front but a bit cowardly really. I expect he'll say it's not his fault when the film's terrible. P.P.S. Everybody on the film, except Red Smith and Cheryl (my nasty aunt – well more silly than nasty really) think as I do. Once more best love from your small friend, Charlotte. P.P.P.S. I hope you're well and enjoying some nice American sun.'

Charlotte finished reading. She looked anxiously at the faces round her. Non-one said anything.

Miranda cleared her throat, 'Well, you certainly covered most aspects.'

'Ever thought of becoming a writer?' Gorgeous smiled.

'Serials would suit you best,' added Ruby.

'I know it is rather long,' Charlotte tried not to look downcast. She and Iris had been up at six writing and had been rather proud of their efforts.

'You were pretty sure you'd get us all on your side then.' Helen took the piece of paper and studied it.

Charlotte looked humble. 'I hoped I would.'

'Well I think it's a wonderful missive,' Gorgeous bounded over to Charlotte and gave her a hug. 'If I was Mr Schute, I couldn't possibly refuse such an appeal.'

'Your first sentence has eighty-six words in it,' Helen said in a wondering tone of voice which then hardened a little. 'I didn't realise you'd seen me trip on the edge of my skirt. You're sharper than you look.'

'I just thought Jo Henry would have done another take,' said Charlotte modestly.

'So we're all agreed it should go just as it is?' said Gorgeous in a business-like way.

'We'll send it to his London office as well as his American.'

'Marked *Private and Confidential*.'

'Very Urgent.'

'Urgentissimo.'

'I know he'll come,' Charlotte sighed, 'It's like fairies. If you believe in them enough they pop out all over the place.'

'Hear that, Gorgeous!' Miranda gave him a hefty nudge.

Chapter 13

THE FILM SHOW

The day after the telegram was sent, Charlotte had a free day. She and Iris returned home with a worrying sense of leaving the scene of action. It would be dreadful to miss Schute's return.

'But he's got to get all the way from America!' insisted Miranda.

'And Concorde doesn't fly to California.'

'I just don't want to miss him,' repeated Charlotte stubbornly. 'You're to ring me at home the moment you hear any news at all.'

'Yes, ma'am,' Gorgeous gave a mock salute. 'Will that be all, ma'am?'

'Yes, thank you. And don't tell Bert. He'd be sure to tell Cheryl and she'd tell Red Smith.'

'Right you are ma'am. Anything you say, ma'am.'

Back at home, Charlotte and Iris shut themselves in their bedroom and refused to come out. They were terrified of giving away their secret to Pansy and Marigold. Pansy and Marigold would be sure to tell Mr and Mrs Leopold just to be mean and then they might feel it their duty to tell Bagelman.

Lily Leopold was quite distressed by their attitude. 'But darling,' she cried through the key-hole, 'we're all longing to hear all about everything!'

'And Dad's taking us all out for pizzas in a restaurant!' shouted Pansy, close behind her mother.

'We're not going out of the house!' Charlotte screamed back immediately.

'Iris, open that door at once,' said poor Lily.

'I think they've both gone mad,' commented Pansy.

In the end they did unlock the door and come out but absolutely refused to leave the house. 'What if they telephoned while we're out,' whispered Charlotte and Iris quite agreed.

Luckily Reggie took a more relaxed view. 'If they don't want to come out for lunch, they don't want to come out. They've probably had too much excitement for a while. We'll bring their pizzas in.'

This view consoled Lily. 'That must be it, poor dears, they're tired and just want a bit of peace and quiet in their own home.' She gave each child a kiss. 'Now just take it easy. We won't be long.'

So Charlotte and Iris sat and watched the telephone during lunch and, it must be said, felt rather cheated when the family returned with stories of ice-cream mountains, and the telephone had not rung.

They still, however, refused to leave the house. 'We feel like a rest,' they said and retired upstairs to their bedroom again.

After about an hour during which the smell of a summer afternoon and the jolly sound of children playing on the pavement outside had become almost unbearable, Iris closed her book and got off the bed. 'I've got to go to the library,' she said firmly.

'What?' Charlotte gave her a reproachful look. But she

knew it was no good arguing. Iris, though the kindest and most unselfish of sisters, could never be moved once she had made up her mind about something.

'My book's overdue,' she explained as she reached the door, 'and I need a new one.'

The bedroom became even more like a prison with Iris gone. Charlotte flung herself on her bed and squeezed shut her eyes. 'I wish, I wish, I wish the telephone would ring.'

The next thing she knew, something had woken her up from a deep sleep. It felt as if an hour or so had past. She sat up quickly and then stood up. The house seemed quiet, empty. Or was that her mother's voice coming up faintly from the kitchen? Certainly no boys. She wandered downstairs.

Yes. Her mother was speaking on the telephone. She could see her through the open door. She had obviously been interrupted making tea. She held a knife in one hand and a pot of marge in the other. Her cheeks were a little

flushed and when she spoke, her voice was high and excited. ' . . . I'm sure she'll be thrilled. We'll both be thrilled . . . No, don't worry at all. I had nothing planned and my husband is home to watch the other children . . . .Oh, we could manage perfectly well on public transport . . . .Well, that's most kind. I much look forward to meeting you too . . . Goodbye.'

She put down the phone and gave a deep sigh of pleasure. 'That is what I call a gentleman.'

Charlotte came into the kitchen quickly. She felt her own cheeks flushing. 'Who was it, Mummy? Who was that on the telephone?' She found she was almost shouting.

Lily looked a little vague. She put her hand up to pat her hair and, since she was still holding the knife, managed to decorate it with a blob of margarine. 'I didn't quite catch his name. Kin, Shoot . . . something. But I wrote down the address. Where you went that late evening once before I wouldn't be surprised.'

Charlotte grabbed hold of her sleeve. 'Schute, was it? An American?'

'Oh yes, he was American. But you'd hardly know it, he was so nicely spoken.'

'What did he want?' Charlotte danced around the room in her impatience.

'He's just back from somewhere – really the way people travel these days, on his way to America . . . '

'Yes! Yes!'

'And since there was a strike at the airport, he's missed his flight . . . He was very nice about you, dear. Very nice . . . '

'But what did he *say?*'

'I'm telling you. So he's in London tonight and there's going to be another little showing of the film and he wants us to go. Most particularly he said. Oh dear, what's that in my hair. Sort of sticky.'

'Margarine,' said Charlotte absentmindedly. The plan was working. He must have read the telegram. What a miracle he'd got back. Now, the question was, should she put her mother in the picture?

Bert picked up Mrs Leopold and Charlotte at 6 o'clock. He gave Lily a surprised look. 'Where's old jangly earrings, then?'

'I presume you are referring to my sister.' Lily gave him a superior look. She was sitting in the back of the car with Charlotte, and did not intend her good humour spoilt by a cross driver. 'Cheryl is not escorting my daughter tonight.' She settled back comfortably. 'You may proceed.' She waved her hand graciously.

'Huh!' snorted Bert.

Charlotte remembered when she and her mother had travelled home in Bagelman's limousine. Really, she thought, it would be too complicated to try and explain everything to her mother, particularly with Bert's big ears flapping. She would just wait and see how things turned out.

The film was showing in the same small cinema where they had seen it before. Halfway up the stairs Gorgeous, dressed in leopard skin shorts and t-shirt, dragged Charlotte to one side, 'I couldn't get away to telephone you. But he's here all right and Bagelman too. Bagelman's smelled a rat and he doesn't know whether to be very charming or cold and dignified. The result is a very funny mixture.' Gorgeous giggled.

'Is Red Smith here yet?' asked Charlotte. She was much the most frightened of him.

'Not yet. But you should have seen him raging around this afternoon. I think he smells a rat too.'

'Do introduce me to your friend, Charlotte,' interrupted Lily, tired of waiting around.

'This is Gorgeous, Mummy. He puts in my ringlets.'

'Well, I can see where she gets her looks from,' simpered Gorgeous. And then added in a quick aside to Charlotte while her mother was still taking in the compliment, 'Don't worry about Red Smith; Julie and Digger have worked out a plan which will literally render him speechless. If he doesn't explode first.'

'Don't you think we should go up, dear,' said Mrs Leopold.

So up they went. Just before they entered the little ante-room, Charlotte hesitated. What if she had been wrong about the American Money? What if he was going to reveal the plotters and blow them all up? Vague memories of Guy Fawkes and The Gunpowder Plot crossed her mind.

'Come on, dear.' Lily pushed her in, 'You must go ahead and introduce me to all your lovely friends.'

The moment Charlotte saw Schute's face, she knew it would be all right. He was turned in her direction and as soon as he saw her, he came striding over.

'Well, if it isn't my small friend!'

He must be referring to the way she had signed herself in the letter. Blushing bright red, she pushed her mother forward, 'This is my mother.'

'Ah, yes. We have already spoken.' He was about the same height as Lily and bent close to her with eyes glowing behind his glasses. Charlotte saw he was a bit of a lady's man. To her surprise, she found herself suffering distinct pangs of jealousy.

'So kind. Such a lovely car. Such a lovely surprise.' Lily spoke with a pleasurable fluttering.

'You know, if your daughter were not such a good actress, I'd say she should become a writer.' His eyes slid towards Charlotte and one of them dropped in a long wink.

'A writer. Well, I don't know . . .'

Charlotte felt a nervous mixture of fear and excitement. 'I hope you didn't mind . . .?'

'Mind what, dear?' Lily was clearly not going to be left out of the conversation.

'Ha. Ha. Your daughter and I have secrets. Film secrets.'

Schute took Charlotte's arm and whispered in her ear 'I was on my way back from Paris . . .'

'Paris!' exclaimed Charlotte.

'Paris,' repeated Lily as if she had a clue what it was all about.

' . . . so it was quite easy to pop in here again and see what the Big Ones are up to.'

'Oh, thank you. Thank you.'

'Well, I must say, Charlotte!' Lily drew back as Charlotte gave the American Money a tremendous hug.

'After all,' Schute straightened up and gave Lily another glowing eye to eye smile, 'Jo Henry's pretty small too.'

'Oh, yes!' agreed Lily with full enthusiasm, as if she no longer cared what they were talking about.

Immediately after this conversation, Bagelman led them into the viewing theatre. There they discovered Red Smith already in position. He lounged very large and very handsome in the middle of the room. At his side was the most dazzling girl Charlotte had ever seen. Like Red, she was wearing a pale blue denim suit. Like Red, she had golden brown skin and huge white teeth and thick corn-coloured hair which, in her case flowed nearly to her waist. They were like a kind of super race, perfectly matched, perfectly healthy and beautiful. Charlotte felt very insignificant indeed. But at that moment she glimpsed Gorgeous out of the corner of her eye. He gave a tug at his own rainbow hair and then nodded towards Red.

Charlotte smiled. She had been so dazzled by Red and his friend, that she had forgotten he was all sham. A wig on top. And sham right the way through to his heart. She settled down more happily between her mother and the American Money. Beyond him sat Bagelman as before and beyond him the young director whose nervousness now bordered on hysteria. As Charlotte watched, he popped a little pink pill into his mouth and, then rolling his eyes heavenwards, popped in another.

Charlotte hoped he wasn't committing suicide but suspected you needed at least a bottleful for that.

The lights went down. Bagelman's cigar smoke wafted in front of the empty screen. Then they were into the ball-room scene. Charlotte had never seen such a mess. After five minutes she had seen more of the back of people's heads than the fronts. After another five minutes she began to wonder if the new young director had a special interest in chandeliers. They seemed to be the stars of the film.

'I can't quite make you out,' whispered Lily.

'I'm the one behind the second chandelier to the left,' Charlotte whispered back.

It was a relief when they left the chaos of the ball-room for the scene outside the house after King Charles' arrival. This time the camera seemed obsessed by their feet.

'I like your little boots,' whispered Lily, encouragingly.

'Sshh, mother.'

'Oh, dear. Poor thing!' Helen had just tripped on her dress. It looked much more ridiculous on film. There was a titter from the back of the theatre. Followed a second or two later by the sound of a door closing.

Looking across the row, Charlotte saw that the new young director's chair was empty. On reflection, she thought it would do him good to commit suicide. At least he wouldn't be able to direct any more films.

The bits continued. Although Charlotte knew that the worse they looked the better it was for their plan, she couldn't help a feeling of depression. All those actors, costumes, film crew working away for nothing. It also struck her that it was one thing getting rid of the new director, it was a second to bring back Jo Henry, but it was quite another to make Red Smith work with him. This horrible thought quite overwhelmed her so that she sank lower and lower in her seat and could hardly bear to look at the screen. There could be no film without Red Smith.

She was roused from her private state of gloom by a

strange sound, half-way between a groan and a grunt. She had heard it somewhere before. She looked up.

On screen, a carriage was just pulling up in front of a grand house.

Oh, no! They were showing the scene of King Charles's arrival. The scene in which . . . Around her she felt chairs creak as people sat up in anticipation. There was Red Smith in full close-up, wearing hat but no wig, looking odd but not too odd.

The groan changed to a strangled cry, 'Stop it!'

The film continued. A footman opened the door to the carriage. Red put his hand to his hat, preparing for his sweeping bow.

There was a commotion behind. Red was trying to get out of his row. No one was helping him. Their eyes were fixed on the screen. He was also trying to take with him the beautiful girl. Who would not leave.

'Stop it at once!' he screamed. No one took any notice. Even Bagelman seemed mesmerised by what he was seeing. His cigar hung limply from his lip.

The hand reached the hat and swept it off the head into a low bow. There was Red revealed in his baldness. Pink, smooth and utterly, completely without hair.

A wild shriek of laughter broke the tense silence. Followed by another and another. Soon the whole cinema was rocking.

Red had fought his way to the door. He could hardly be heard above the noise. 'I'll murder you! I'll murder you all! You'll never work again! None of you!'

No one took any notice. They were all enjoying themselves far too much. Archibald, the greyhound, now appeared on screen jaws a-tremble with Red's luxuriant wig. Red's face of horror as he realised his hairlessness caused a new wave of hysteria in the cinema.

Then the chase was on. The playful, leaping greyhound and the frantic stumbling man.

In the end it became painful to laugh any more. The noise in the cinema lessened and those who had fallen to the floor in their paroxysms got up. The American Money wiped his eyes and although the chase was still on he looked down at Charlotte, 'Quite a revenge,' he murmured, 'Quite a revenge!'

'I didn't know about this,' hissed Charlotte.

'Ah, so the whole crew were all behind you.'

They were interrupted by a new sound. An ugly tearing, wrenching, vibrating. The screen suddenly went blank.

'Red's found the film booth,' commented Schute.

'I didn't know it was a comedy,' said Lily in a rather bewildered voice.

Red Smith appeared in the doorway. The lights went up. Everyone blinked dazedly. In his hand he held up a mass of dark coils.

'Medusa's head,' said Schute.

But Charlotte could hardly make out what it was. She looked round at the faces in the cinema. They all looked quite drained with laughter. Some very pale, some very red, many stained with tears.

Red shook the dark coils. His voice was like a knife scraping a plate. 'I have the film,' he said. 'Here in my hand. No one will ever see that film again. Ever again. Not any part of that film. That film is a dead film. That is the end of that film. It is no more.'

There was a complete silence. Charlotte noticed that Schute was reading a note that had appeared from somewhere.

The silence continued. Then Red's girl-friend snickered. She tried to stop herself. She failed. 'But Red, you looked so funny, so funny,' laughter threatened to choke her. 'When I think how well I know you, I thought I knew you' more laughter, 'and to think I never knew, I never guessed, you never told me, I mean you're *famous* for your beautiful hair – that it's all a fake, a sham and that really you're, you're,' she was again stopped by laughter, 'you're absolutely and completely *BALD*!' Tears of laughter poured down her face.

'I'll strangle you! I'll strangle you with this film. I'll . . .' Red bounded forward so ferociously that Julie and Digger jumped up to restrain him.

He stood between the two of them, struggling and screaming.

Lily Leopold leaned across worriedly to the American Money. 'Isn't he pleased we all laughed?'

'Apparently not,' Schute stood up. He said loudly but calmly, 'I think it is time you and I had a private talk, Red.'

Beside him Bagelman, who had kept very quiet up to then, mumbled, 'Disgraceful incident, perfectly disgraceful.' But since his fat and ugly face was still creased with laughter and his eyes were all red and squeezed, no one took much notice.

The American Money walked over to the still-struggling Red. He said something softly and showed him the note. Red went noticeably pale and stopped trying to escape. He looked at the film still clutched in his hand and dropped it to the ground. He seemed to have entered the tranquillity of despair. Julie and Digger let go of him.

Schute put an arm round his shoulder (Red seemed to have shrunk since the evening began) and led him out of the viewing-theatre.

Just as Red passed the door, he gave one last cry: 'Blackmail!' he shouted and was gone.

Chapter 14

TOO MANY TEARS

The reason for Red's sudden change of humour was soon explained to Charlotte. The film which they had watched, and which he had captured so triumphantly, was only a copy of the original negative. That was safely hidden and would only be released to him on condition he finished making the film with Jo Henry.

It was indeed blackmail. But, as everyone agreed, under the circumstances quite acceptable. After all, it was only his ridiculous star's vanity which made him terrified of the world knowing he was bald. Any normal person would have simply joined in the laughter and that would have been that.

So it was his own fault. But Red needn't worry too much. The film crew would not show the film to anyone else. Indeed they'd forget all about it. As long as he behaved himself.

The filming started again three days later. It had taken that long to discover Jo Henry who had gone to bury his sorrows in an equatorial rain forest. He was apparently considering making a film with the gorillas of Rawalpindi, feeling they might be more amenable than humans.

Charlotte was a little disappointed in Jo Henry's lack of gratitude. He strode about the house in his usual energetic way, criticising the furniture, the costume and even the food.

'We got better bacon sandwiches in the jungle!' he shouted on the second morning.

Soon the old-style grumblings began. 'He made me stand completely still for TEN minutes!' wailed Helen Wittering, 'And he wasn't even filming me.'

'I can't run with a 150-pound light on my back,' groaned an electrician.

'A gorilla could,' replied Jo Henry.

'We are not gorillas!' cried at least three people.

In fact the only person who didn't grumble at all was Red Smith. He appeared exactly as needed, performed his part carefully and then left. Neither Bagelman nor the beautiful girlfriend had appeared since the famous film showing. He was on his own.

'Serve him right,' said Gorgeous.

'It might improve his character,' commented Miranda.

'No chance of that,' Ruby tied a white satin bow in Charlotte's hair. 'Now remember she's not really dying.'

They were about to film Lady Clarissa's death scene. Everybody was worried about how this might upset Charlotte. Charlotte, herself, was not at all worried.

'How can I cry and be all upset unless I think she really is my mother?' she asked in a reasonable tone of voice.

'But we don't want you to get too upset.'

'I like being upset,' she replied staunchly. 'It's fun!'

No one could think of any comment on that.

The bedroom, where Lady Clarissa was to die, was very grand indeed. In the centre stood a huge four-poster bed. It was hung round with heavy brocade curtains. Helen was propped up on a pile of cream silk pillows. Her face had been made up to look exactly the same colour. Dark circles had been painted all round her eyes and her hair drawn tightly back into a little cap so it looked as if it were cut short. The curtains at the windows of the room were drawn and the only light came from four fat candles set high on long brass candelabras.

'Perfect!' Jo Henry announced to Julie in satisfied tones, as Charlotte came into the room. 'This should have tears flowing like the Ganges.'

Charlotte stood by the great oak door waiting for instructions. She felt very happy, very full inside, ready to weep as fast as Alice in Wonderland. She didn't understand the bit about the Ganges. In her left hand she held a white embroidered handkerchief.

Jo Henry began to talk to Helen. He bent closely over her but Charlotte could still hear his excited voice and see his hands flying about. He was telling Helen how to act. Soon it would be her turn. Charlotte noticed how he talked to each actor in turn, never all together. It made each one feel special.

'Well, well, well, well!' Jo Henry crouched down in front of her. 'So here's my clever little telegram writer.' He took both her hands in his, 'I never did say thank you, did I?'

'I expect you were too busy.' Although Charlotte's heart burst with pride she tried to put on a grown-up's voice of understanding.

Jo Henry laughed. 'You are forgiving.'

'Actually it was great fun. You should have seen Red's face when he saw his wig in Archibald's mouth!'

Jo Henry bent nearer, 'As a matter of fact I did,' he whispered. 'But don't tell anyone. The only reason Red can bear to work with me is because he thinks I don't know his awful secret.'

'He is silly.'

'Quite.'

Jo Henry drew back a little. He took up the end of the handkerchief. What's this?'

'A hankie. For crying into.'

'Ah.' He looked at her seriously. 'You're planning to do a lot of crying?'

'It is my mother dying.'

'Quite.' His expression remained solemn.

'I did hear you saying about flowing tears,' added Charlotte defensively.

'I was thinking about the audience's tears. Not the actors. If the actors cry, the audience won't feel the need. The actors must try very very hard not to cry however much they feel like it.'

'Oh.' Charlotte twisted her handkerchief. She had really been looking forward to bursting out with huge sobs. She had imagined her blue eyes shining through pools of glinting tears.

'You must keep it in here,' Jo Henry taped her tummy. 'And then it will all be terribly sad. Right?'

'Right.'

'Good girl.' He stood up. His voice changed. 'You will walk in the door, see your mother obviously very ill, react, run to her bedside, stop at the white mark, curtsey, and then wait.'

'Yes, Jo Henry.'

'O.K. To your positions. And complete quiet please for a rehearsal.' Digger shouted and they were off.

Charlotte thought she was gradually learning a quite different attitude to acting. She began to see that being a film star meant a lot of hard work and not much of it very glamorous. On the other hand, there was nothing more exciting than when it went well and she managed to please Jo Henry.

He was very pleased with her that day. He said her expression of love and sorrow when she forgave her dying mother could not have been equalled by Elizabeth Taylor in *National Velvet*. Charlotte only knew this was a very special compliment by his tone of voice, and it was Ruby who explained she was one of the great film actresses.

At last it was the end of the day. Charlotte let her dress fall off her body to the floor. She felt quite exhausted. 'Can I cry now?' she asked Ruby.

'Of course, darling,' Ruby opened her arms and Charlotte threw herself on her ample bosom and cried and cried and cried.

She was interrupted by Cheryl's shocked voice from the door. 'There! I knew this dying mother bit would be too much for her. Come to Auntie Cherry, Charlotte.'

Charlotte lifted her tear-stained face. It wore a blissful smile. 'I've never felt so happy,' she said. 'I can't tell you how wonderful it is to be crying!'

'What?' Cheryl grabbed a chair and sat down. She looked at Charlotte suspiciously, 'People cry because they're unhappy.'

Ruby smiled sympathetically. 'Not film actresses, dear. They're different from other people. And your niece is turning into quite a little star.'

'Not a star, please.' Charlotte wiped her face with the white embroidered handkerchief. 'There, I'm better now. Come on, Cheryl, let's go and find something to eat.'

Taking her bemused aunt's hand she danced them out of the room.

As it turned out that was one of the very last days they spent filming in the grand house.

'It's the tourists,' Gorgeous explained. 'And the greedy owner. Every year the house is opened to them the first week in September, next week. Charabancs come from all over the place, huge parties of tourists, there's a dancing festival and an exhibition of Queen Victoria's underwear. They all pay to see the garden and the house and Sir Elsinore makes pots of money.'

'So he won't let us finish filming here next week,' asked Charlotte.

'He wants us to pay all the money he'd get from the

tourists. Or out. We should have been finished if it hadn't been for all the Red Smith problems.'

'Filming seems one long problem,' Charlotte sighed. 'So what will we do?'

'Studio,' Gorgeous picked up two pairs of cherries and stuck one over each ear. 'We'll finish the outside stuff here and then go inwards.' He stood up and did a little shimmy, 'You'll find studio life, dear, not a bit like being on location.'

Charlotte had a weekend at home before they moved to the studio.

Her mother bustled about her anxiously, 'I'd never have let you do all this filming if I'd known it would last so long.'

'I've never been in such regular employment,' Cheryl anounced with satisfaction.

'Do you realise Charlotte starts school the week after next? She should be at home, playing with her brothers and sisters, resting, not gallivanting all over the place.'

Charlotte didn't say anything. She knew nothing could stop her finishing her part in the film now.

'And such extraordinary people too,' added Lily who had never got over the wild scenes in the viewing theatre.

'Actors are very emotional,' explained Charlotte patiently. She had decided it was not worth trying to make her mother understand all the ins and outs. Her father would have understood. But he was going back to his tanker in a few days and was very busy with preparations.

'School is much more important than acting,' said Lily in a firm voice as if it was something she had been thinking about.

'Yes, Mummy,' Charlotte kept her voice low. 'I've got an article in a magazine to show you. It says our film "heralds a new glamour in British film-making".'

'Well, I must say!' Lily was obviously impressed, despite herself.

No-one had explained what a studio was to Charlotte. She had assumed it was a single large room with a glass roof like artists used. She was therefore amazed as Bert drove them into a whole town of what looked like large garages of the sort Fred and Ned stored their toy cars in. They were connected by all sorts of passage-ways, covered and uncovered and separated by narrow roads criss-crossed with arrows and other automobile instructions.

Bert threaded his way to a small green door with professional ease. 'Ah, it's good to be home!' He hopped out enthusiastically.

'I don't know about home. It's like a blooming maze.' Cheryl looked round nervously. 'I'll never find my way round.'

Bert held his arm out gallantly. 'Never say Bertrand Plum abandoned a damsel in distress.'

'Two damsels,' Charlotte got out of the car and stood behind her aunt. Cheryl seemed rooted to the spot. She stared at Bert.

'Albert. That's what I thought. Mrs Albert Plum. That I could consider. But Bertrand. Bertrand. Well, what sort of name is that?'

'A distinguished name. That's what sort of name Bertrand is. Not a common or garden name like Albert.'

Charlotte now also stood transfixed. 'Mrs Bertrand Plum.' Did that mean . . .? She remembered her mother saying that Cheryl would never be satisfied with any man for a husband, not with her combination of grand ideas and sharp tongue.

'Bertrand. Bertrand. It does get to sound rather aristocratic after a while. Sir Bertrand . . . .'

Charlotte thought she'd heard enough. 'When you engaged couple,' she rang out the words, 'have finished I've got some work to do.'

Ordinary cars would be like toys in this garage, thought Charlotte, as they entered, it was so very large. Of course it wasn't really a garage.

'You're to go straight to the set.' Bert took Charlotte's hand and she thought True Love had made him kinder.

The set gave Charlotte a surprise. It was exactly like the drawing-room of the grand house. Except that one side was wall-less, cut open. This allowed the cameras to move in and out. 'It's even got those pretty flowers on the ceiling,' Charlotte looked up wonderingly.

'It's an exact replica, dearie,' Ruby came bustling over, 'but I wouldn't push the walls too hard or you might put your hand through.'

'Can I go inside?'

'Quick then. Jo Henry wants to do your nightdress scene.'

'The one where I jump out of the window? And run to warn King Charles about my mother's evil intentions?'

'You do know a lot today.'

'If I didn't know the story by the last week's filming, I'd have to be pretty stupid, wouldn't I?' Charlotte walked into the drawing-room. She looked for the window she must jump out of. There it was, a tall, many-paned window above a padded seat. She then remembered something else. 'But I already jumped out of the window and ran across the lawn. That's why I knew about it.'

'I expect Jo Henry wants to film you from inside the room.'

'Well, he certainly couldn't film me outside.' Charlotte leant through the window. There was a brick wall, many ropes of electrical wiring, several large lights (possibly brutes) and various bits of scenery.

Ruby joined her. 'Oh, they'll put a garden backcloth up so you'll seem to be jumping towards lawn and flowers. Come on, now.'

Charlotte allowed herself to be led away. 'I suppose I'll have a mattress to jump on.'

'I shouldn't worry about that. They won't want their young star to break a leg.'

They reached Ruby's dressing-room through a maze of green corridors.

Charlotte stuck her arms up for Ruby to lower the white lacy nightdress. 'It's all a cheat, isn't it?'

'What?' Ruby's mouth was full of pins.

'I mean none of it's real. None of it. Not the room, the garden, the people ... I mean I'm supposed to love my father, but he's Red Smith whom I hate and who hates me. And everyone will think I have lovely ringlets and actually it's Gorgeous spending hours with curling-tongs.'

'Well, that's films, isn't it, dearie?'

'Making people believe in the unreal? Cheating them?'

'I wouldn't put it quite like that. I mean they know they're watching a film. They want to believe it. Otherwise they wouldn't watch.'

'That's true.' Charlotte sighed. 'I feel as if I've grown up so much during this film. When I started it was like playing. But now it's like ... I don't know. Not playing anyway.'

'Work,' said Ruby, giving her nightdress a final pull.

Ever since his return from the Rain Forests Charlotte had made a point of checking on Jo Henry's state of mind. Lately, he had returned to the small weaselly look he had at the beginning of the picture. He shouted more than ever or walked into corners muttering and only talked to Charlotte just before a scene in which she was to act.

His smallness, she thought, was partly due to the size of the building in which they worked. She soon discovered there were other films being made at the same time as theirs. When they went down to the huge canteen, there were other directors, other cameramen, other actors. They were no longer special. A self-contained family.

Julie sat at another table gossiping to friends on a different film. Gorgeous showed off to a bevy of admirers. Helen had found a boyfriend and Red Smith was always surrounded by groups of fans or suede jacketed executives.

Only Jo Henry sat alone, his face getting sharper every day.

One lunch-time Charlotte took her courage in both hands. She bought a fresh orange juice which she knew he liked and went over to sit by him. He looked up with a start.

'I bought this,' Charlotte pushed over the juice.

He didn't seem to notice it. 'Four and a half more days,' he muttered. 'Even doing full over-time there's no way we can do it.' He slammed his fist on the table. 'If we don't finish, the film's a dead donut. The best film I've ever made. And that makes me a donut too. Bagelman's just waiting his chance to get me. Like a great fat vulture. Schute's all right. He's done his bit. But he can't do any more. They'll get him too if this fails.' He looked up and round the room wildly. 'And what do we do? Have tea-breaks, lunch-breaks, supper-breaks! And no one cares.' He slumped back into his seat again. 'No one cares.' His head dropped onto his chest.

Charlotte put a timid hand on his sleeve. 'I do.'

'Er. What?' His red-rimmed eyes peered absently.

'I care. I care about the film.'

The eyes cleared and focused. 'You care, do you?' A very faint smile lightened his face. 'Was I rambling on there?'

'You seemed very worried about not finishing the film.'

'I am.' Jo Henry frowned but not in the horrible distracted way previously. He came even nearer to a smile. 'You care about the film, do you?'

'Yes. Definitely. And it's not only me. Every one cares. It's just that they have friends here. You can't blame them for that. But they care very much indeed.' Charlotte used her most school-mistress voice. 'So you see you are quite and absolutely wrong. And moreover I have no doubt at all that if you stopped shouting or muttering and just behaved sensibly, though, of course, at speed, I have no doubt at all WE will finish the film on time.' Charlotte pursed her lips and gave him a severe look. 'And if that happens I wouldn't mind guessing it will be a HUGE SUCCESS!'

Jo Henry stared. He put his hand to his head. Then he let

out a huge bellow of laughter. It echoed round the room. Charlotte tried not to be embarrassed though she could imagine every-one looking.

'Just behave sensibly. . . .' roared Jo Henry. 'Isn't that what you said?'

Charlotte decided she might as well continue. 'When you shout all the time, it slows things down.'

Jo Henry managed to control his laughter. 'I don't know what I'd do without you,' he said. 'There must have been magic in the air the day I picked you. You hadn't any experience like the others. But there was something about you . . . . So you think I can finish if I stop shouting and behave like a normal human being.'

'If possible.'

'We'll make it possible.'

Jo Henry raised the cup of orange juice, 'To *Ladies and Gentlemen* and Elizabeth, without whom it wouldn't have been possible.'

Charlotte tried hard not to be conceited about it but she had to admit to herself that from that moment, things seemed to move forward much more smoothly and speedily.

Jo Henry was in such a good mood that she even felt able to take him up on his promise to let her family visit the filming.

It was the morning of the last day. She had expected to be sad. But with Ned and Fred and Pansy and Marigold and Iris and Mrs Leopold, all bursting with excitement, it was difficult to be anything but excited too.

'Now,' lectured Charlotte, as they arrived at the studio, you know I have to work and so does everyone here, very, very hard because we're behind schedule.'

'What's behind schedule?' asked Pansy.

'Late,' continued Charlotte, 'so you must be very, very quiet and do exactly what Digger . . .'

'What's Digger?' asked Marigold.

'The Third Assistant,' answered Charlotte.

'What's the Third Assistant?' asked Lily.

'It doesn't matter,' Charlotte smiled kindly at her mother and sisters. They looked back at her with admiration. 'He's a man covered with wires. He'll look after you or pass you on to someone else. Just do what you're told,' here she turned on the twins fiercely, 'and don't touch anything.'

She needn't have worried. They were all much too over-awed to touch anything.

They stayed till lunch and were then driven back home again by Bert.

As they went Pansy whispered to Charlotte, 'They must have had an awfully big lorry to move that bit of the house over here.'

Charlotte smiled but didn't explain. It was nice knowing things other people didn't. Particularly when the other people were her older sisters.

Chapter 15

LAST SCENE

They were shooting the very last scene of the film. Of course it actually came from somewhere in the middle of the story. There was an air of tension in the studio. Eleven more minutes and after that the lights would go dark and the cameras stop turning and the sound stop recording.

Helen, Red and Charlotte were all in the scene. Elizabeth was trying to explain to her father that her mother was planning to betray him. She was interrupted by Lady Clarissa herself. Elizabeth had two lines.

'Please, papa, spare me a moment. Mama is meeting some men.' At which point Lady Clarissa swept in and kissed her husband lovingly on both cheeks.

By now Charlotte was professional about timing and emotion. But she still found words difficult, particularly when addressed to Red. He had a way of looking at her as if she were some kind of disgusting insect. He shifted his shiny black boots as if ready to stamp on her. It made it particularly difficult to concentrate.

Also, a large crowd had gathered to witness the last scene.

Designers, set-dressers, prop men, grips, electricians, chippies (carpenters), extras, stand-ins and even Bernard B. Bagelman. He sat in one corner on a very large chair with PRODUCER written in very large letters. His cigar smoke wafted over the set despite a notice just above his head saying NO SMOKING.

Charlotte felt sure he would like her to make a fool of herself. Which she seemed well on the way to doing. At first it was the 'p's in 'Please, papa, spare . . .' There were somehow too many in it they came in the wrong places. She found herself saying 'Please, papa, stare . . . .' and then 'Peas, papa, pare,' and then 'Please, ta ta, tear.' Poor Jo Henry was very patient but she could see the desperate way he glanced at his watch. They had to have this scene in the film and they had to finish, in, now, nine minutes.

'Please, papa, spare me a moment.' Wonderful she had said it.

'Yes, my child, speak your mind.' Red narrowed his eyes in obvious derision. The next line was 'mama is meeting some men.' Charlotte knew it very well. She opened her mouth confidently. Out came the words:

'Papa is making a pen.'

There was a horrified silence. 'Cut!' shouted Jo Henry, 'prepare to go again at once.'

'SILENCE please,' screamed Digger.

'Yes, my child, speak your mind,' repeated Red, this time with a curl of the lip.

Charlotte took a deep breath, 'Tomorrow Pete is ten!' She stopped aghast. Where had these words come from?

From somewhere at the back of the set, there came a strangled cry. Desolate under the bright lights, Charlotte was just able to see the writer bent double as if in pain. This was the first time he had reappeared since Jo Henry's sacking.

'Just try and start with "Mama"' whispered Jo Henry, 'the rest is sure to follow. We have three minutes and your mother still has to burst in.'

Off they went again.

'Yes, my child, speak your mind.'

This time Charlotte avoided looking at Red. 'Mama,' the word slipped out easily, 'is treating her hen.'

A huge guffaw went up from round the set. Waves of laughter buffeted Charlotte where she stood sweating under the bright lights. 'I'm sorry,' she murmured, 'It's Red.' But only Red heard.

'Serves you right, Miss Know-all!' he hissed under his breath. 'You're about as much a film actress as I'm the President of the United States.'

'O.K.' shouted Jo Henry. The laughter died. 'We'll dub her lines in. Come on now Helen. Let's try for an immediate take.'

And suddenly, after all the anguish and excitement, the filming was over.

Charlotte, feeling deep in disgrace, wondered what dubbing her lines meant. But before she could ask anyone, she found herself caught up in a whirl of dancing bodies. From nowhere she was surrounded by smiling faces, friendly hands, Gorgeous, Ruby, Miranda, Helen, Julie, King Charles I, Digger, Jo Henry, and even the writer. All kissing and hugging and laughing and crying out: 'We've done it!'

'We've made it!'

'It's all finished!'

Somehow behind it all she had an image of Red Smith and Bagelman going out together like two huge red turkey-cocks.

But then drink appeared, bottle after bottle, and food, great mounds of chicken and sausage and cheese and cream cakes and a bowl of strawberries so big that it had to be set on an especially strong table.

Charlotte found herself a chair and went to sit beside it. She decided to try and see if it was possible to eat so many strawberries you didn't want any more.

Bert and Cheryl found her as she popped the forty-fifth into her mouth.

'Drowning your sorrows, eh?' Bert winked.

'What do you mean?' Charlotte looked at them suspiciously.

'End of the movie, dear,' Cheryl gave a smile that reminded her of Red. 'Back to school on Monday. No more fun. No more special treatment. Just one of a class at school, one of four sisters at home. Quite a come-down for our little film star.'

Fortified by strawberries, Charlotte smiled upwards 'Not at all. As a matter of fact I shall be needed for dubbing shortly.'

'Oh,' Cheryl looked at Bert for guidance. Clearly she knew no more about dubbing than Charlotte.

'That is on the cards, of course.' Bert nodded sagely. 'It's actually post-syncing. They re-do all the fluffed lines and suchlike. Just sound into a microphone and then lay it over the picture.'

'So you see,' Charlotte sucked number 49, 'I'm not finished at all.'

Despite Charlotte's brave words, it was a terrible moment when the time came to say goodbye. For one thing all the adults had consumed such large quantities of alcohol that they hardly seemed able to concentrate on her leaving. In fact they hardly seemed to be able to stand up or put sensible words together.

Charlotte thought they looked very silly, red in the face and reeling around. She was feeling rather sick now, having proved at number 111 that you can wish never to see another strawberry again.

'Goodbye, Jo Henry,' she said, holding out a polite hand, 'thank you for having me on the film.'

'Not-at-all!' He made the words run together and clapped her so hard on the back that she nearly fell over.

'Mama is laying a hen, eh! Ha! ha! *HA*!'

'I'm sorry,' said Charlotte in a small, hurt voice.

'Not-at-all,' repeated Jo Henry. 'All come out in the rub-dub-dub eh? That's good. All come out in the rub-dub-dub!' And he caught anyone nearby to tell the line again and roar with laughter.

So Charlotte gave up formal goodbyes and giving a baleful look at Gorgeous, who held a glass in either hand, and Ruby, whose face was almost lost in a giant slice of cream cake, and Miranda who, for some reason, was standing on her head, she left the set.

'I don't like film parties,' she said to Bert when she got in the car.

'They're always the same,' Bert took seriously his job of driving the car and therefore remained sober. 'Too much drink, too much food and a lot of silliness. Like silly children really.'

Charlotte sat up straighter. 'Not at all like children,' she said in a dignified manner. 'Children would never behave like that.'

'That's rich,' Cheryl gave a giggle which turned into a hiccough. She had not felt the need to join Bert in his self-restraint. 'They're behaving like adults, then, are they?'

'Yes,' said Charlotte bitterly, 'very silly adults.'

Chapter 16

POST-SYNCING, DUBBING AND EDITING

Perhaps it was just as well Charlotte turned against the film company at the end. For, as Cheryl had pointed out, there could be room for only one thing in her life now: school!

On Sunday evening Charlotte opened her cupboard and took down her uniform. It was grey. Grey socks, grey cardigan, grey sweater. About as far as you could get from Gorgeous' rainbow hair or Ruby's tasselled table-cloth or Jo Henry's fringed suede. . . . Banishing these bright images, Charlotte picked up the skirt and held it against her. The hem barely reached her knees. It must be time for her to inherit Pansy's.

Perfectly on cue, Mrs Leopold entered the room with a couple of Pansy's skirts over her arm.

Under her arm was a long envelope.

'What's that?'

'It's for you.'

Charlotte opened the envelope carefully. She hadn't had a letter since her last birthday.

'It arrived by a messenger on a motor-bike.'

Inside the envelope was a piece of white notepaper and a yellow slip. On the slip were written the words 'Pay Charlotte Leopold one thousand pounds' and then in numbers '£1000'.

Charlotte looked up at her mother. She felt quite dazed. Lily, thinking it bad news, took the slip from her. She read it.

Mother and daughter looked at each other. Then Charlotte broke out laughing. She snatched the paper and danced around singing, 'I'm rich! I'm rich! I'm very very rich!'

Lily laughed, too, and then she took Charlotte's hand and said quietly, 'I'm very proud of you. You're a very special girl. And you deserve every pound.'

And Charlotte felt so happy she wanted to cry but instead she said, 'It's for you, Mummy, so you can buy that run-about car you've always wanted.'

And then Mrs Leopold looked as if she was going to cry. So it was just as well they were interrupted by Ned and Fred, who were too young to understand the importance of money.

'We'll put it in the bank,' said Lily, 'until we can find just the right car.'

So that was how it was left and Charlotte buttoned up Pansy's grey skirt and thought that she could never fit back into school routine with money like that in the bank.

But the strange thing was that by the end of her first week at school, Charlotte felt as if she had never known any other life. She had told her close friends about the film but they had been only superficially interested, not caring to know the details. Charlotte realised it was so remote from their own experience that they couldn't be bothered to make the effort to understand. It was an exciting idea, to be in a film, but not part of real life, not to be taken seriously.

Miss Bracken, the music teacher who hit you with a cymbal if you didn't attend, was to be taken seriously. Mr Goethler, the art teacher who hung Samantha upside down to explain action painting, was to be taken seriously. Above all, Miss Doughty, their form teacher who believed the whole school was in a plot to kill and eat her pet dachshund, had to be taken seriously. In fact, so serious was her case that she was shortly removed from the school altogether which meant several weeks of very odd supply teachers. With so much going on, it was hardly surprising the film world became a misty dream to Charlotte.

It was a full five weeks before Charlotte heard anything more from the film company. Then Mrs Leopold received a short type-written letter announcing a date on which Charlotte would be needed for post-syncing. (Still, neither of them knew what the word meant.) Since the date was during the week, Charlotte had to get permission to miss school.

On Wednesday afternoon was their 'Drama and Movement Class.' Charlotte was very cross to miss it. 'Silly old post-whatting,' she complained, 'I was planning to act Cleopatra on her burning barge. Now Henrietta will do it instead.'

However, the moment Bert appeared with his car and started talking about 'the art of post-syncing' in a knowledgeable way, she saw things quite differently.

Suddenly their 'Drama and Movement' became a silly childish game and the film world was the only thing worth working for. It was very odd, she thought, how the two worlds could only exist one at a time. And when she was in one the other quite disappeared.

The dubbing theatre was frightening. To get in they had to go through two soundproof doors. In the space between them, it was perfectly silent, like death. Inside the theatre, it was dark, quiet too. And then suddenly a screen at the far end burst into life and there she was in glorious technicolour, a golden sunlit figure dressed all in white with her face framed by a mass of curls. 'Mama is treating her hen,' she said sweetly and then the screen went black.

There was a slither of laughter and then Jo Henry's voice, loud in the darkness. We'll do that bit last. It can't be sync. anyway. It'll probably have to be over Red. Hasn't that girl arrived yet?'

Charlotte cleared her throat. 'I'm here, Jo Henry,' she said nervously. It seemed unlikely he would even recognise her in all the grey uniform as the same girl who had just performed so glowingly on the screen.

'Come on over then!' As Charlotte's eyes got used to the dim light, she saw that on the other side of the theatre was a glass booth, rather like a telephone kiosk. It had some lighting inside which enabled her to see Jo Henry holding the door open.

'Ta, ta. I can see you're in good hands,' Bert went, breaking her last contact with the outside world.

Charlotte made her way over to the booth.

'Well, well, well. You do look a little grey mouse. Come on in. Now what we're doing is very simple. You just stand here behind this light. And when it goes red you'll see a bit of film come on the screen. And underneath that is a line of moving green blobs moving from left to right. When it reaches the far end you say your lines into the microphone here. Is that clear?'

Charlotte looked up at him in despair. It was not clear. It was like at the beginning of the film when he issued orders and expected her to follow them without understanding.

'Is that clear?' he repeated, his impatient energy even more obvious.

Charlotte took a deep breath. 'No,' she said.

'Ah. I see.' Jo Henry stopped bouncing about and seemed to consider her seriously for the first time. 'Would you like to see how it all works?' he asked in a quite different sort of voice.

'Yes,' said Charlotte.

So Jo Henry took her hand and led her out of the glass

booth to the back of the theatre. There he introduced her to a nice man called Bob who sat at a desk covered with buttons and knobs.

'He's controlling the whole show,' explained Jo Henry. 'Recording your lines over the right bit of picture.'

After that they went up into another bigger glass booth where the projector which directed the film onto the screen buzzed gently.

'Now do you feel better?' Jo Henry led her downstairs again. They arrived at her booth.

'Yes, thank you, but . . '

'But, what?'

'How do I know what I'm going to say if I'm concentrating on little green blobs on the bottom of the screen?'

Jo Henry laughed. 'Four reasons: firstly, they're lines you've said a million times before during filming; secondly, you can hear yourself saying them as often as you like on screen before we go; thirdly you've got the script in front of you; and fourthly, I shall tell you what they are over these headphones here.'

Jo Henry bent forward and took a pair of headphones from the table. 'Now you put these on. I go out and shut the door which means you are in a completely soundproof atmosphere. Your words will come over absolutely clean of background. I shall go back to the controls and talk to you. You can only hear me over the headphones but I can hear you whether you speak into the microphone or not. Right? Clear? O.K.?'

He had taken so much trouble to explain that Charlotte didn't dare admit how nervous she still felt. However, she did ask one more question as he stood at the door, ready to leave. 'Why? Why am I doing the lines again?'

'Just to get them better.' Jo Henry was casual. 'For one reason or another. Lots of actors have to do it. It's part of the film actor's art.'

Charlotte sat in the little phone booth all on her own –

apart from Jo Henry's voice coming over the headphones. 'O.K. This is the line "You look so elegant, mama", I want to give it a feeling of loving surprise as if it just pops out of your mouth unprepared. Watch the green blobs. And don't worry, this is only a rehearsal.'

So there they were back to the very first line Charlotte had ever said, all over again. All over again. 'You look *so* elegant, mama'. 'You look so *elegant*, mama.'

Charlotte thought that no one who hadn't been involved in a film could possibly appreciate how much hard work went into making it. Quite apart from the dramas. Everything had to be done over and over again in all sorts of different ways. It was as if Miss Doughty had made them write school essays ten times. And, mad though she was, she never made them do that.

In fact after the first quarter of an hour she began to enjoy post-syncing. It was rather like a computer game, watching the moving green blobs and then coming in with her line.

Eventually she got to the problem piece of dialogue, 'Mama is meeting some men.'

'O.K. said Jo Henry into her ears. 'Don't think about it, just say it.'

And to her amazement, that's what happened. No problem at all. Her ears began to reverberate and she realised he was clapping.

He came running down to the booth. 'Terrific! Better than most adults. I expected to need you all day but now it's only lunch-time and we're through. Well done!'

'I enjoyed it, actually.' Charlotte smiled a trifle smugly.

'I'll tell you what,' Jo Henry took her arm, 'do you want to see how a film's edited? I'm going there now. Shall I take you as a reward?'

'Oh, yes please,' said Charlotte enthusiastically, although she had to suppress a sneaking longing for lunch. Jo Henry's plans seldom included food. On the whole, he considered it a waste of time.

'That's settled then. An extra afternoon's editing. Just what I needed!'

Charlotte followed Jo Henry along narrow garishly-lit streets. The late September sunshine seemed out of place on the dirty pavements and tawdry shop fronts.

'Soho – Den of Iniquity!' Jo Henry exclaimed. 'Cover your eyes, ye pure in heart!'

Charlotte blinked and rubbed her eyes. She had not yet got used to the brightness after the dim dubbing theatre.

'I'm here!' With his usual briskness Jo Henry whisked her through a doorway and up some narrow stairs.

Suddenly they were standing in a large glaring room. All round the walls hung shiny pieces of film. Some were short, curling at the ends like snakes raising their heads, others were long, dropping down into silver bins.

Three men were in the room. One sat at a long table. In front of him was a screen about the size of a television. In front of that, laid along the table, was a strip of film and a strip of something else that looked like tape. As he moved the film backwards and forwards a picture appeared and disappeared on the screen.

Ed got up from his chair. 'Go on. Sit down. And I'll show you how it all works.'

Charlotte sat down. Ed put her finger on a button. 'Press this.' The film came up on the screen. 'You can make it go backwards or forwards. Slow or fast.' He showed her how to do it. 'The second tape is the sound.'

Charlotte ran the picture forwards and back. It gave her a very odd feeling. To be in control of people in this way. She looked at the screen. It happened to be the scene where she jumped out of the window, shot from the outside. She made herself jump back in very quickly and then jump out again very quickly.

'And then we just snip off and stick together,' said Ed, 'it's all very simple.'

After she jumped out of the window, Red appeared and caught her in his arms and held her lovingly. How odd it was, thought Charlotte, watching it in slow motion, that he looked so warm and comfortable and handsome. When he was really so horrible.

'I hope you've chopped out a lot of Red Smith,' she said still staring at kind blue eyes.

'Certainly not!' Jo Henry took the controls from her brusquely and ran the film fast forward so that there was more of Red laughing gaily. 'He's giving the performance of his career. I don't want to cut a frame.'

'But he behaved so evilly,' stammered Charlotte, 'getting you thrown off the . . .'

'Sshh,' interrupted Jo Henry. 'That's all past.' He stilled the film, a close-up of Red, and smiled at Charlotte, 'People have done worse to me.'

'Making films is a rough business,' said Ed, also smiling.

'However, it does have compensations.' Jo Henry stood up and led Charlotte towards the door.

Lunch, she thought, he's going to take me out for a slap-up lunch.

'It seems, if all goes well with the final edit, *Ladies and Gentlemen* has been chosen for the Royal Command Performance.' He took Charlotte's hand. 'How do you like that? Your first film having its first performance in front of the Queen!'

Chapter 17

ROYAL COMMAND PERFORMANCE

One Saturday morning not long after Charlotte's visit to the cutting-rooms, Mrs Leopold received an enormous envelope. Since it was breakfast time, all the children stared with curious admiration at its size and its whiteness.

'It's probably a Death,' said Lily but her eyes glittered excitedly.

Even Ned and Fred were quiet as she slit it open. She pulled out a square card the size of a small poster. Craning their necks, the children could see it had a brightly coloured picture on it and some writing in heavy type.

'Where's my glasses?' A flush was rising in Mrs Leopold's cheeks. She held the card a yard from her face and read with difficulty. 'You . . . are . . . invited . . . to attend a . . . Royal Command Performance . . . of *Ladies and Gentlemen* . . .'

' . . . which will be graciously attended by Her Majesty Queen Elizabeth II,' finished Pansy reading at great speed over her shoulder.

'Well, I don't know.' They all sat back, quite stunned by the news.

'I told you so,' said Charlotte smugly, 'and you wouldn't believe me.'

'Her Royal Gracious Majesty,' murmured Lily, picking up the card again.

'Who is commanded to attend?' asked Marigold, recovering her voice, 'You and Dad? And Charlotte? Or all of us?'

'I don't know. It doesn't say.' Lily became flustered. 'It says Evening Dress, Medals will be worn.'

'Oh, look!' cried Pansy. 'There's something else in the envelope.'

'Darling, be careful!'

But Lily warned too late and a flutter of blue tickets fell to the floor. Ned and Fred crawled under the table: 'Here's one!'

'I've got two!'

'That's mine!'

'No, it isn't!'

'Yes, it is.'

'Sshh! Children, please,' Lily's voice rose above the confusion. 'Ned take that ticket out of your mouth. Fred hand those to me.'

In a second or two Lily had all the tickets safely in her hand. She began to count. 'One, two . . .'

'That's Mum and Dad,' commented Iris.

'Three, four . . .'

'That's Mum, Dad, Charlotte and Iris.'

'Cheryl,' said Mrs Leopold, 'five, six . . .'

'That's Mum, Dad, Charlotte, Cheryl, Iris and me!' screamed Pansy excitedly.

'Seven, eight . . .'

'That's Mum, Dad, Charlotte, Cheryl, Iris, and ME!' yelled Marigold.

There was a pause. 'And Ned?' asked Iris.

'What about me!' shouted Fred who had no idea what was going on but wasn't used to hearing Ned's name without his.

'Nine,' Mrs Leopold stacked the tickets in her hand. 'The whole family. To go and see the Queen of England.' She sighed dreamily.

Charlotte was a little put out. 'It's my film you're coming to see.'

Her mother patted her hand. 'Yes, dear. Of course. And that's why Her Majesty is coming too.'

'Do you think she'll bring Lady Di?' asked Pansy, who had a collection of Princess photographs.

'I shall have to have a new dress,' announced Marigold, firmly.

'We'll all have to have new dresses,' agreed Pansy.

'What date is it?' asked Iris.

'I shall have to bring my new car,' said Ned.

Mrs Leopold looked back at the card. 'December 16th. Just perfect. The end of school term and your dad will be home. Even if he hasn't got any medals he looks lovely in his tanker captain's uniform.' She paused and looked up. Everybody could see she had tears in her eyes. 'December 16th will be the happiest day in my whole life.'

Charlotte, the cause of it all, looked down modestly at the remains of her boiled egg.

Mr Leopold lined up his children in the living-room. He would have liked to have Lily to help but she was far too busy trying to persuade Cheryl to leave behind an ermine cape she'd found in an antique shop. They could hear her exasperated voice, 'You don't have to compete with their Royal Majesties, you know!'

It was the evening of 16 December. Six o'clock. It was dark and a slight snow fell outside the misted windows of the living-room.

'That's right, Pansy, stand straight now.' Mr Leopold stood back to take a proper look at his eldest daughter.

'I'm not a sailor, you know.' Pansy, being so tall and thin had been the hardest to find a dress to suit Lily's sense of a royal occasion.

Remembering her success as a page boy in the film, Charlotte had suggested she dress as a boy. This had made Lily very cross. 'It is not a joke,' she rebuked her sternly.

In the end a red velvet jacket and skirt once belonging to Lily had been cut down to fit her. Pansy and Marigold, being so near in age and both having short dark curly hair, were wearing identical blue tartan dresses with white collars.

'So who's Tweedledee out of you two?' asked their father, moving down the line.

'Oh, Daddy!' pouted Marigold. 'It's all Mummy's stupid idea to dress us the same.'

'She wants people to be amazed at two sets of twins!' complained Pansy.

Neither girl had been quite sure they wanted to be dressed the same as the other and now they began to look distinctly rebellious.

At that moment Lily entered pushing a cross-faced Cheryl in front of her. 'There!' she cried, 'Doesn't your silly aunt look dreadful draped in all that moth-eaten fur?'

The children looked at her consideringly. Then Charlotte opened her mouth. She chanted 'Bye baby Bunting, Daddy's gone a-hunting. Gone to fetch a rabbit skin to wrap his baby Bunting in.' And all the children began to laugh (Except Ned and Fred who had been zipped into such tight little navy blue suits that they could hardly move or speak. 'And don't think that's accidental,' Lily had commented to Charlotte as she zipped them in. 'I'm not having them spoiling your evening with their pranks.')

Soon Reggie and Lily had caught the laughter from their children. Lily wiped her eyes, 'Oh, dear, oh, dear. My mascara will be down my nose.'

'I'll kill you!' screamed Cheryl rushing at Charlotte who had started it all. But her silver shoes had such high heels that she twisted her ankle and half-fell. She hopped about angrily. 'I'll tell Bert not to bring that limousine he's taken all the trouble to get!'

Everybody stopped laughing. They were all very much looking forward to travelling to Leicester Square in a limousine.

'I'm sorry, Aunt Cheryl,' Charlotte stepped forward. 'Can I help you with your shoe?'

'No!' snapped Cheryl.

Lily came up. 'Oh, darling.' she said in her special warm voice, 'What's that glittering on your finger?'

This provoked an immediate transformation.

'I thought you'd never notice! It's my engagement ring. Bert gave it me this morning.' The coat dropped to the floor and was forgotten.

The girls, keeping the matter of the limousine in mind, crowded round with enthusiastic admiration.

'It must have cost a bomb!'

'Sapphires and diamonds too!'

'He must love you desperately!'

Charlotte stayed a little apart. She was wearing a long white lace dress with a wide pink satin sash. She had never felt more beautiful. It was her mother's wedding dress. It had been lifted from the box under the double bed where it had lain ever since Charlotte could remember.

Cheryl had said she'd never cut up her wedding dress. But Lily had been determined. 'I want it to meet the Queen!' she declared, obstinately.

Charlotte was the only one of them who was to be actually presented to the Queen. She wore long white gloves to her elbows so that the Queen wouldn't get her hands dirty.

Charlotte drew back a flap of living-room curtain. She saw her own reflection, the pink satin ribbons in her hair, the string of corals that had arrived for her from Bernard Bagelman. (That was odd. Did he think he could get round her to forget his bad behaviour? However she couldn't resist wearing them.)

'What are you staring at? Has the car arrived?' Pansy's voice interrupted her.

She looked past her face in time to see an enormous black car draw up in front of the house. 'Oh, no! It's a funeral car!'

Everyone rushed to the window. 'It is! It's a hearse!'

Bert was let into the house by Reggie. 'I said I'd get you a big one and that's what I did.' He sounded sulky.

'I think it's splendid!' cried Lily, who was determined everything should be splendid.

'Bags I be the body!' joked Reggie.

'We'll all fit in very nicely,' said Lily even more firmly.

It was cold outside. The girls huddled into the red velvet cloaks Lily had made from curtain material. Bert threw his arm round the ermineless Cheryl. 'You're my star!' he cried.

They drove into central London. As they reached Marble Arch the few flakes of snow increased and became a whirling mass of white. Ned and Fred, despite their tight suits, managed to shriek with excitement: 'Can we go sledging! Let's make snowballs!'

Charlotte didn't take part in any of this. She kept her face pressed against the window. She was the first to see the cinema. She could tell it by the crowds gathered on the pavement outside and by the lights glaring into the snow. This was her world, the world of film.

Bert began to pull in. All around there were rows of policemen wearing the smart stripes of the metropolitan force. Two stepped out and tried to wave the huge hearse on.

Pansy and Marigold began to giggle. 'He thinks we've lost our way to the crematorium.'

'Oh, dear.' Even Lily sighed as Bert began shouting through the window.

'I've got a star in here! And her family. All *bone fide* first night audience.'

'Show him the tickets, Lil,' suggested Reggie who was never put out by social inconvenience.

'It's so embarrassing,' Cheryl tried to hide her face, 'in front of the crowds and lights and everything.'

And even Charlotte, despite her euphoria, felt a blush rising.

However, after much scrabbling in her new evening bag, Lily produced their tickets and the police reluctantly let them into the curb.

'I told you so!' Bert jumped out indignantly and rushed round to the door. 'I might have had royalty in here,' he growled to the nearest policeman.

'On their way to the next kingdom, I've no doubt,' replied the policeman. And the crowd, hearing the interchange, broke up with laughter.

None of this spoilt their entrance into the cinema for Charlotte. She let the others go a little ahead and then followed head high. Camera lights flashed all around. As she crossed the threshold into the brilliantly lit foyer, she heard a woman say, 'That looks like the little girl in the poster.' She inclined her head in what she hoped was a royal and gracious smile. Another flash-light popped.

Inside the foyer they were met by a group of elegant men dressed in black suits and black bow ties. 'Can I help you to your places, sir?' one approached Reggie politely.

'My daughter here's in the line-up to meet Her Royal Highness,' said Reggie bravely. Even he was feeling a bit overwhelmed by the occasion. And Lily, Cheryl and the other children were almost completely silent. Only Pansy dared whisper to Marigold, 'There're no other children here.'

They were told to go up to a second foyer on the next floor. All around them glamorous men and women in full evening dress pushed up the stairs, staring round and chattering. Charlotte recognised none of them. She nudged her father, 'Who are these people? They don't come from the film.'

He smiled. 'They're your audience, sweetie. Come to see the stars.'

But then on the next floor, Charlotte began to see people

she knew. Red Smith was the most obvious. Unlike everyone else he was wearing a white jacket and a black drooping bow round his neck. His blonde hair gleamed in the lights. On his arm he had a blonde girl in a tight scarlet dress, who was very like the girl he'd brought to the film showing, yet not exactly her. As Charlotte watched, he was led away to a little roped-off corner of the foyer. He disappeared into a concentration of lights and photographers and microphones.

'That's where they interview the stars,' whispered Cheryl. 'Let's go over.'

But just then another usher approached Reggie. 'Can I help you to your seats, sir?'

Lily produced the tickets and they were moving as slowly as possible to the entrance to the cinema when Pansy noticed Charlotte wasn't with them. 'She was here a minute ago,' Lily looked round helplessly.

'We have to get you all seated before their Royal Majesties arrive,' said the usher not very patiently.

'Oh, there she is!' Iris pointed. 'With Helen Wittering and Red Smith.'

The usher looked. His expression changed. 'She's part of the film is she?'

'Oh, yes.' Lily beamed proudly. 'She's called Charlotte Leopold. She has an important part in the film. She's going to be presented to Our Gracious Queen.'

The usher became anxious in a different way. 'Well, why didn't you say? You don't go to your seats. There's a special place for you to stand and watch the presentation.' He hustled them off to another corner.

'But what about my daughter?'

'She'll be looked after.'

In fact at that moment Charlotte was being led over the ropes in front of the television cameras.

'Miss Leopold,' the television interviewer glanced down at his clipboard. 'You're very young and you've never been in a film before. How did you find it acting with such a famous star as Red Smith?'

Charlotte paused. She looked at the camera's round eye. A terrible temptation to tell the truth took hold of her. How very badly he'd behaved and how very bald he was. But just then she caught sight of Jo Henry in the crowd. She remembered what he'd said in the cutting-rooms about Red's brilliant performance, and the importance of the film above everything.

So she gave her sweetest smile and said demurely, 'I was very honoured to work with such a great actor, and I learnt a tremendous amount from him.'

There was a little ripple of appreciation for such nice sentiments in the crowd around and then she was led out of the ropes and Jo Henry taken in.

The interviewer consulted his clipboard again, 'Mr Jo Henry, this is the first film you've directed for three years. Were you surprised when it was chosen for the Royal Command Performance?'

Jo Henry didn't hesitate. 'When you have such magnificent talents as Red Smith, Helen Wittering and all the others who have worked so hard to make my dream turn into reality, then anything less would be an insult.'

'Well, congratulations!'

Behind them the presentation line was forming up. The foyer had cleared considerably and now Charlotte could see Bernard B. Bagelman in a very shiny evening suit that rippled over his fat form like a snake's skin. Next to him stood Red Smith, Helen Wittering and there, looking particularly small but very elegant, was Mr Schute.

'Look, there's the American Money!' Charlotte waved happily, as she and Jo Henry were led over to join the line.

'I sure approve of that,' the American Money touched a flap of Charlotte's white lace.

'It's my mother's wedding dress,' confided Charlotte. 'She wants it to meet the Queen.'

Schute gave such a loud laugh that everyone looked round and the Chief Usher said loudly, 'Sshh! PLEASE.'

The Queen was on her way. They all became very, very quiet. There was a sound of cheering coming from outside the cinema. Charlotte felt her heart beating painfully. It would be terrible to faint in front of your sovereign. Her mother would never forgive her.

Then the Royal Party was up the top of the stairs and at the top of the line. Suddenly everything happened very fast. In quick succession Charlotte found herself at very close quarters with four faces who she knew better than her own. The first generally was seen on postage stamps and was fringed top and bottom by such an array of glittering jewels that she could hardly focus on the features. She swept into a deep curtsey and came back up just in time to hear the mouth say, 'Well done. What lovely fun you must have had!' The Queen moved on.

The second gave her a manly shake and said 'Jolly good!' He was smaller than she'd expected. He was the Duke of Edinburgh.

The third was quite unexpected. She was young and very pretty, surrounded not only by jewels like the first, but frills as well. She said, 'I wish I could have Red Smith for a father!' Princess Di is jealous of me, thought Charlotte in a daze. The fourth, followed close on the third, particularly as she approached Red. He said nothing to Charlotte but gave her a very white smile. He was the Prince of Wales.

Then it was over and Royalty had gone and Jo Henry had gone and the American Money had gone. She was back with her family and they were being whizzed into their seats. Lily was crying slightly with the emotion of it all. 'I want to die,' she repeated ecstatically until she was drowned by twelve trumpeters of the Household Cavalry who signified the arrival of the Queen.

Everybody stood up and they played a stupendous fanfare.

'That's what I call music!' murmured Reggie, approvingly.

'I like their jockey caps,' whispered Pansy. And Lily's tears began to roll even faster.

They were just going to sit down again when 'God Save The Queen' roared out.

'With HER actually present!' sobbed Lily. Everybody else sang very energetically to show their patriotism. At last they were all settled down. Charlotte couldn't help worrying that the actual film might be a bit of an anti-climax after so much excitement. The lights dimmed and the movie began. Red Smith, a glorious hero, in flowing cape and feathered hat, came galloping through the trees. . . .

Now was Charlotte's best moment. Here it was in front of all their eyes. The film she'd helped to make. And it was good. It was exciting. She could tell by the way her sisters watched and Cheryl and her father. Her father, particularly. He very seldom went to films and when he did tended to shift around a lot and look at his watch. But she could feel he was caught, wanting to know what happened next.

And it wasn't just because she was in it. They were just as interested when she was off the screen.

Charlotte leant back in her chair and smiled into the darkness. It was going to be a success. A right royal success.

Two hours later the story drew to its sad yet noble end and great waves of applause filled the cinema. Even the Queen's departure did not distract from the audience's enthusiasm. They clapped and cheered and stamped.

Reggie tapped Charlotte on the shoulder, 'Not at all bad, my girl,' which was high praise from him.

'I loved your dresses,' said Pansy which was high praise from her. 'Although I can't see why they needed you filming for so long when you were only in half the scenes.' Which was more like her usual attitude.

'Less than half,' argued Marigold. And soon they were all putting their points of view and only the twins, who had been asleep since five minutes after the film started, were quiet.

It was hard not to feel a sense of let-down as they joined the crowd pouring outwards. However the sight of Gorgeous dressed in a white silk suit with a black shirt and white bow tie did cheer up things.

Charlotte introduced him to those of her family who didn't know him. And soon he was joined by Miranda Watson-Poxson and Ruby and Julie and Digger and various other members of the crew, with all their wives and husbands or boyfriends or girlfriends, until they were filling most of the downstairs foyer. 'If you don't mind, ladies and gentlemen, please,' the ushers said, trying to move them out of the cinema.

But that only made them even jollier. 'Yes!' they cried, 'That is the name of a very good film, I hear: *Ladies and Gentlemen*!'

Soon the twins had woken and were running round between all their legs causing added confusion. So Gorgeous said to Charlotte, 'Since the bigwigs have left you'd better bring your lot on to a first night party we're having.'

And Charlotte was about to say yes when she remembered the end-of-film party. And how they'd all become drunk and like silly adults.

So she said, 'No, thank you very much.' And they all kissed emotionally and said good-bye.

Collecting themselves together, the Leopold family headed for the glass doors leading to the pavement. There they could see the wild figure of Bert waving them to the left.

'He's probably parked on a double yellow line,' said Reggie.

'At least they'd never tow away a hearse,' said Cheryl.

Charlotte gave one last look over her shoulder. Gorgeous caught her eye.

'See you on the next film!' he cried.

'Yes! Yes!' cried all the others, see you on the next!'

'Yes,' whispered Charlotte as the glass doors shut behind her. She looked up at the black sky, no longer filled with snow-flakes but instead decorated with a myriad of glittering stars. 'Yes, please!'